DUST ON THE HEATHER

OUTBACK SKYE

BOOK 2

HEATHER REYBURN

For my wonderful writing friends, Susan, Phillipa and Michelle

Thank you

1

March 2025

Unseasonally icy rain thrashed against Helen Gooding's legs as she peered into the grave, her heart seesawing between shock and euphoria.

A comforting hand rested on hers.

'Are you ready to go, Mum?' Lisa asked. 'I'm freezing.'

Helen waited for the minister to disperse the first clod of dirt before turning to face her daughter. She nodded silently, gripping Lisa's hand while begging her thumping heart to settle.

An arm encircled her, and she leaned her head momentarily against her son's shoulder. Tall, solemn and the image of her dead husband, Tim otherwise bore no similarity to his father and for that she was grateful.

'Steve's fetching the car,' he said. 'We need to go. The crowd will be getting restless at the hall.'

Helen glanced down at her watch. Almost five o'clock. She would have to endure another two hours of this charade before she could escape. Food and drinks would flow, hugs and kind words would be shared. But beneath it all, Helen doubted there would be a single person truly sorry to say goodbye to Jack—except perhaps the blonde bimbo her friend, Shelley, had seen him with the previous week. There wasn't much Shelley missed, and although usually a reliable secret-keeper, sometime over the years she had spread a protective wing over her neighbour. Now she shared anything she considered Helen should know on the off-chance Helen would do as Shelley recommended and leave the man. So once again, receiving the news of Jack's infidelity had been accepted by Helen with a resigned twist of her gut.

Gritting her teeth, Helen allowed her shoulders to sag a little farther and added another layer of loathing to her already frozen heart.

An exhausting three hours later, the four of them collapsed onto the faded, worn lounge suite—her two strong, loyal sons and equally reliable and beautiful daughter with not a tear between them.

Helen ran her hand over the thinning leather,

remembering the day she had bargained for their furniture at a nearby clearing sale. Nothing in the Elizabeth Downs homestead was new, or smart. But it was clean and well cared for and had served the family well. Surrounding the shabby, weatherboard home, new sheds and yards told a different story—the bright green tractor dominating the machinery shed, the jewel in the crown.

'So what's next?' Steve asked, slinging a long leg over the arm rest and running a hand through his freshly trimmed mop of curls. 'If you're okay here, I'd like to get a head start at dawn tomorrow. Gotta lot of work lined up now the wet is over.'

'Me too,' Tim added, staring at his phone. 'Willooga Station are mustering and want the trucks on standby to start carting as soon as possible.'

Helen swallowed her unease and fixed a smile on her face. Both her sons had fled the home farm as soon as they could, eager to work for anyone other than their father. And while Tim had been delighted to be taken on by a trucking business, working his way from washing vehicles to managing the fleet, Steve had stumbled from properties in both Victoria and South Australia to the wild, untamed Northern Territory. There he'd discovered a passion for flying helicopters and now he was the proud—and often stressed— owner of a contract mustering-by-air company.

Lisa, several years younger than the boys and the

animal-lover of the family, had dreams of qualifying in veterinary science. But with no funding for university, she had settled for vet nursing instead. She adored her work in a large animal hospital based on the Sunshine Coast—often thankful for the 1000 kilometres separating her from her childhood home and her father.

Helen's back stiffened with remorse. How could she tell them? After all the years of putting up with his erratic behaviour, narcissistic personality and terrifying temper tantrums, Jack had betrayed her. The secrets that, as part-owner of the farm, she should have known about ... and had some control over.

'Cup of tea anyone?' Lisa asked brightly.

'Please,' Helen said, relieved to have more time before she divulged the truth.

'Me too. I need something comforting inside me after listening to people sprouting on about how wonderful he was,' Steve said bitterly.

'How come no one knew him like we did?' Tim said with a flinty sneer.

A silence laden with unspoken memories settled on the room, lifting only as Lisa arrived bearing a tray of steaming mugs and a container of peanut brownies.

Helen sipped a mouthful of tea then placed the mug on the coffee table. Unable to eat, she reflected on her newly widowed state.

For almost forty years, the man in the coffin had been her husband—and now her sentence had been served. Had he ever been a friend? She wanted to think so, at least in the early years anyway. But somewhere in the fog of protecting a run-down farm from financial ruin, bearing three babies, and farewelling not one but both her parents following terminal illnesses, their relationship had changed—and so had he. All she'd learned the previous day had wiped away any remnants of love, friendship or respect from their relationship, and the ongoing police investigation did nothing to ease her predicament.

'I've bad news I'm afraid.'

Three pairs of eyes met hers—Tim's narrowed and wary, Steve's wide with surprise, and Lisa's hooded with fear.

'Are you about to tell us it wasn't an accident? That the weaselly Warren Peck finally saw Dad's true colours and did something about it before he did a runner?' Tim grunted.

Helen shook her head. 'I'm quite sure it was an accident but regardless, I'm leaving that to the police. Hopefully the truth will be revealed. I know Warren isn't the most likeable person, but at least he's been able to work with your father—unlike those who've been here before him.' She drew a deep breath, bracing herself for the response. 'No, it's something none of us ever thought we'd face; we have to sell Elizabeth Downs.'

2

'What?' Tim said, leaping to his feet. 'It's productive—at last!' He shook his head in disbelief. 'Now that Dad's gone, you can employ someone to help you or consider share-farming. Either way, you'll have no trouble making enough for a good life. It's what you've worked so hard for, Mum. This is your chance—and after all the rain we've had, it's looking good.'

Helen raised her eyebrows. 'I agree. It does look nice and to be fair to Warren, he's had a lot to do with that—no doubt hoping to feather his own nest but ...' Helen's voice broke, fury and despair enabling the tears she had held back all day to trickle down her cheeks.

Lisa jumped up and wrapped her arms around her. 'Mum. Tell us what's happened?'

Helen cleared her throat, removed a ragged tissue from her pocket and dabbed her eyes. 'As you know, I met with Mr Booth, the accountant, yesterday before you guys got home. He apologised. Said he discovered the true situation in the last couple of days and was mortified. I couldn't lay blame on him. Actually, I felt sorry for the poor man. Over the past couple of years, it seems that somehow your father was able to hide the true financial facts from everyone.' She paused, biting back her anger as the frowns deepened on her offspring's faces. 'I don't know how and I'm not sure when this began, but if Jack hadn't died, goodness knows what would have happened. Selwyn Booth is almost eighty, but your father insisted we stick with him because he'd looked after us for decades. Now we know why. It's my own stupid fault.'

Fury welled again and she clenched her fists as she continued.

'Like you all, I believed what your father told me ... that with Warren's help, the farm was entering easy street thanks to tweaking the loan—and the purchase of the new tractor. Huh! Yes, the tractor has made a huge difference in being able to get essential jobs done with ease. But tweaking the loan was an understatement. We were looking at the most prosperous year we've ever had.' She stopped, biting back the nausea crawling up her insides.

'So—what's changed?' Steve asked.

'It was all a lie! I believed your father and had no idea of the debt he'd accrued. He insisted on managing the farm accounts without my help. His reasons are now clear.'

'Which were?' Tim demanded, his voice deepening. 'The debts, I mean.'

She named the exorbitant amount, unsurprised at the audible gasps from her children.

'Your father forged my signature! He used my name to borrow money.'

'From whom?' Steve paced up and down the worn floorboards. 'Surely Mr Booth has all the information?'

Helen shrugged. 'He does but I admit I was so shocked when he told me, I didn't think to cross-question him about the details. All I could think about was the years I've slaved on this place. Planted hundreds of trees, carted water to skinny stock through years of drought, worked as hard as every shearer in the shed— and continued to run the house and vegetable garden so at least I could put decent meals on the table. The worst part is your father was so fixated on becoming the "Lord of the district" he pledged everything we own and never considered how hard it would be to repay the debts. Now they're so huge there's not a hope in hell of me clearing them without selling everything. And I'm sorry—I know I'm being pathetic—but I'm so angry!'

'So ... you're sure there'll be nothing left? Not even

enough for you to buy something smaller elsewhere?' Steve said, incredulity thickening his deep voice.

'No. Nothing for any of us—and I know you've got your own careers, but I always thought one or more of you might eventually return and things would improve.' Helen slumped into the couch, spent. Tears trickled down her face once again and no one said a word for a long minute.

'Mum. Don't blame yourself—or worry about us.' Steve rested his hand on her arm reassuringly. 'I don't think any of us want to live here again. It's not only because of Dad. It's just not where we want to be—and there's not enough happy memories to pull us back again. I'm looking at buying my own place in the Territory, and ...' He looked at his brother. 'Tim and Heidi have already bought property in Longreach. I'm sure it won't be long before Lisa finds somewhere she's happy to put roots down too. Now you've told us all this ... truth,' he waved an arm around as though attempting to encompass the entire farm, 'it's clear we have the freedom to fulfil our dreams. It's you who needs help.'

'Thanks, Steve.' She raised her head, her eyes hooded in thought. 'If we can get out of this without owing anything, I'll manage somehow.' Her mouth twisted in a wry smile. 'My two afternoons a week in the restaurant aren't exactly a manager's wage, but it's better than nothing and I've managed to squirrel away a bit each week that your father never knew about.'

'Good grief,' Tim said, rubbing a palm across his face. 'What a mess. How did none of us see this coming? We were pleased—relieved to see Elizabeth Downs looking so good. I don't want to leave things like this.'

'Something will work out. But in the meantime, I'll talk it over with Mr Booth and the solicitor and begin putting sale plans in place.' From deep within her, a rod of strength surfaced. She squared her shoulders. The last thing she'd wanted to do was reveal the truth but there was no way she could keep anything of this magnitude to herself. In some ways, she felt engulfed in relief. Caring for a large outback property with all it entailed and all who relied on the management of it depended on sheer hard work and a lot of luck. And it looked like the Gooding family had run out of that— big time.

'Have a chat with Clint, Mum. He's honest, friendly and efficient, and he'll have a good handle on valuations,' Steve said. 'We'll get together again as soon as we can and until then, touch base by phone.'

Helen nodded, tucking a lock of hair behind her ear. Clint was an old school friend of Steve's who had set up business in the rural real estate industry. His confidentiality and tactful management of clients was well known.

Lisa stood and loaded the tray with the empty cups. 'I'm owed a few days off, so I'll stay and help get this sorted.' She spoke firmly, her pretty face stern and resolute. 'What Dad has done financially is despicable. But ... he's dead now, so hopefully nothing will have a chance to deteriorate further.'

Her determined glare swung from her brothers to her mother, and she added, 'We're here for you, Mum. Elizabeth Downs will be sold and the debts kept quiet. This is your chance to get out of the district and I'm sure everyone will understand when you tell them you want to make a new life elsewhere.' She lifted her chin, her tone firm. 'The autopsy report supports an accidental death, and we can only hope the police do too. We'll cut our ties here and hold our heads high.'

Helen nodded, warmed by the shared support from her beloved children. For years she had dreamed of ways to leave and begin again—but not once had a suspicious death or bankruptcy featured in even the wildest of her musings.

3

———————

*H*elen barely slept, recalling the statistics she had heard on the radio only days earlier—that the fastest growing group of homeless in Australia was now women over fifty. It chilled her to the core. Very soon, she may be one of them. In between snatches of sleep and the possibilities of her future, she'd had frightening, distorted dreams. She was alternately crouching, hiding, running, and finally, leaping from a cliff top into a deep, dark hole.

With the last terrifying vision, she woke fully, sat up, and took deep, slow breaths.

They're nonsense dreams—all part of your overactive mind and the stuff you're trying to process.

She looked up, picturing her husband's face laughing down at her. Her body stiffened, filling with rage. *And you are not going to finish me, no matter how hard you try.*

Faint light filtered through her bedroom window. She pushed the dark images away, focused on the misty view over her garden, and switched her mind toward the practicalities of what was to come. She had never been a hoarder, so clearing the house would be easy. The children had progressively removed their belongings, and she kept only the basics and her two most precious possessions—her sewing machine and a stash of well-read books. For the first time in her life, she was relieved she never had the money for anything but a meagre, mostly home-made wardrobe of cloth-ing. A small drawer of jewellery, makeup, and precious little trinkets her children had made for her over the years would fill no more than a shoebox.

It was too early to consider where she would go, but wherever that might be, she had enough to begin a new life.

Perhaps I'll be able to rent something with a garden— somewhere to grow flowers?

It was a dream she had buried for decades. With the exception of a rambling bougainvillea and a few precious geraniums, flowers had been a luxury. Feeding the family by growing her own vegetables and making a living from the farm to cover everything else had taken priority.

She sidelined the flower-growing thoughts and

focused on other possibilities. As a practical person, she had experience in a wide range of activities and skills. Driving vehicles of any type, cooking—she could possibly get a job on a large property requiring a cook? She shook her head. Perhaps not. Too close to home. Years of employment as kitchen hand at the local restaurant had provided her with more cooking tips and tricks than she could have dreamed of, but even with the wage the work provided, the hot, steam-filled kitchen in temperatures of forty degrees held little appeal.

A chuckle burst from her. Jack had never accepted her mathematical talents. She was certain that was why he'd refused to allow her to touch the farm accounts—he couldn't bear to be the underdog. Her retail skills were honed, stimulated by many years of her once-a-month voluntary assistance in the community charity shop where her natural aptitude for spotting a bargain and meticulous record-keeping were appreciated.

Her shoulders sagged. *And look where that's left me.*

Minutes passed before she dismissed her negative thoughts and smoothed the sheet. 'That's behind us now.' She spoke softly. 'It won't help to dwell on the negative.'

A wave of anxious pleasure surged through her. *I'm a widow.* A new beginning? It offered the freedom she had dreamed of for years and yet fear and guilt had held her back. She wasn't sure why she'd felt guilty. Was it because when she'd married Jack she had promised to obey? Grunting with disgust, the brief wave of delight disappeared. She tossed back the blankets and stepped onto the cold, bare boards.

I've been weak. Pathetic. Old-fashioned and stupid. But I was also pregnant with Tim.

Her thoughts were disrupted by a gentle knock on the door before Steve appeared.

'Come in.'

'I've boiled the kettle. Are you ready for a cuppa?'

'Love one. I won't be a minute. Let me get dressed and I'll join you.' Helen returned his warm smile before he closed the door behind him, and she opened the wardrobe.

Within minutes, the four family members were settled at the kitchen table, hands wrapped around hot drinks as a quiet resignation surrounded them.

'I've made a to-do list,' Lisa announced. She cast a quick glance around the family and continued. 'Mum and I will go to town today and visit Mr Booth and the solicitor. We'll ring you both this evening with the update. We'll also have a chat with Clint. I'll ring him and see if he can come here if he's not in his office.'

Tim nodded. 'Good idea. Before I leave, I'll take photos of the machinery and equipment and do some research on valuations.'

Helen heaved a sigh as she stared at the empty

veranda. 'I've missed old Dusty but now I'm relieved she's gone. Shelley will welcome the chooks, but I would have hated not being able to keep Dusty. Finding a job and a house to rent somewhere will be difficult enough and if animals were part of the deal, it'd be even harder.'

'I'm sure it won't come to that, Mum,' Steve said. 'Let's take one step at a time.'

Helen pushed her chair back and shared a resigned nod. 'Righto. Breakfast first then you boys can get away and I'll nip out and check the cattle. Thank goodness we've sold the weaners.' Her chin lifted a little and she smiled. 'You know what?' She paused for a few seconds while her children caught her gaze. 'You're right. Everything will work out.'

Lisa chuckled, and both men grinned at her. 'Ever the optimist,' Lisa said.

'We're here for you and although it might take time,' Tim added, 'I believe you'll be okay.' He looked at Lisa. 'Meanwhile, if you don't mind throwing some breakfast together for us, Steve and I'll do a quick audit of the sheds and be back in ten.'

The atmosphere lifted as a new, lighter sense of confidence filled the room.

'Mum,' Lisa said. 'I'll feed the chooks if you do the cooking?'

Helen shared a smile with her daughter and pulled

the frypan from the cupboard. 'Your wish is my command!'

A GOLDEN SMUDGE of sunlight hovered on the western horizon when Helen and Lisa crossed the cattle grid onto Elizabeth Downs late that afternoon.

'For once I'm pleased to be home,' Helen said.

'Yeah. We've covered a lot of ground today and I feel better knowing what actually has to happen.' Lisa grinned. 'How lucky were we to catch Clint banging that sign in on the edge of town? He's such a nice guy and it was good to hear he's positive about buyers. Thank goodness the drought's eased and people are actually wanting to buy farms.'

Helen nodded thoughtfully then gathered the folder of papers from the back seat. With a cautious spring in her step, she crossed the dusty yard.

As the women entered the kitchen, the phone rang, its raucous tones filling the silent house.

Helen hurried across the room and grabbed the handset. 'Hello?'

'Helen, it's Lucy.'

'Oh Lucy, how lovely to hear from you.'

'I'm so, so sorry. We've been flat out with lambing, and I haven't had a chance to catch up with my emails until now. I was devastated to read the news that Jack has died. Are you alright?'

Helen sat on a kitchen chair and pressed her palm against the speaker. *'It's Lucy,'* she mouthed as her gaze met Lisa's.

Lisa nodded and pointed to the back door. 'I'll lock up the chooks and let you catch up,' she whispered.

'I'm fine, Lucy.'

There was a moment's pause. 'Okay. You don't sound like yourself. Are you sure?'

Helen breathed out a sigh of resignation. 'We've known each other a long time so I'll be honest. No, I'm not quite okay yet—but I will be.'

'I understand. The grief of losing your partner after so many years together must be awful. I know how hard it was after Robert died—and we hadn't been married nearly as long as you and Jack have. Is there anything I can do?'

Helen bit her lip. Although she, Lucy, and Roslyn had been friends since boarding school days in Toowoomba—a lifetime ago-their communication had been largely via phone calls on special occasions and exchanging birthday and Christmas cards. Now Lucy spent most of her time on the Isle of Skye with her adoring partner, Fergus.

A chortle threatened and Helen swallowed it, her lips switching.

Ironic that this is kind of another special occasion. My freedom.

'Thanks, Lucy. There's nothing you can do but it's good to be able to talk to someone who understands.' She straightened her shoulders and drew a breath. 'Marriage isn't always as good as we think it will be. Jack was a difficult person, hard on the children as well as me, and I should have left years ago—but I didn't.'

Her friend's empathy was evident as Lucy responded quietly, 'Roslyn and I always wondered. Are you happy to share more with me?'

The beep of an incoming call came through as Lucy finished.

'Umm. I am but could I ring you back? Things are a bit hectic here.'

'Of course. Let me know when you feel like talking. I'll always be here for you,' Lucy said.

Helen bit back a tear at Lucy's words. Regardless of the traumas she'd suffered in her own life, Lucy had been one of those special friends who never judged, never interfered, but was always there when anyone needed her, especially her best friends. Except for Shelley, Helen didn't have many. In her voluntary and paid work, she'd been professional but private—at least as much as she could be in a small, rural community. Her home life had none of the atmosphere she wanted to share with other women, so she'd never opened her home to friends and rarely accepted invitations that didn't include the family. That would have ignited nothing but trouble. But she had never minded. Happy with her own company, she preferred to remain private—even if anonymity was impossible.

'I've got a call coming in and I need to take it. Would you mind if I rang you back?'

'That would be great. Talk whenever you get a chance.'

'Thanks, Lucy.'

Their call disconnected and she switched to the incoming one.

'Hello?'

'Hi, Mum.' Steve's voice sounded muffled, as though he was in a cave. 'Can you hear me okay? I'm not in a good service area but couldn't wait any longer to hear what happened today.'

'I can hear you, but I'll be quick in case the call drops out.'

'Righto.'

'The situation is as we thought. Debts are ridiculously high ... but here's the good news. Clint said the sale possibilities are good. He doesn't believe we'll have too much trouble selling.

'Oh. So he's getting onto it?'

'Yes. He's sure it's a good time to sell—especially while this place has never looked better.'

'Perfect. What did the accountant say?'

'Everything hinges on what we can get for Elizabeth Downs. I don't want to be greedy but after speaking with Clint, I believe we'll be offered a fair price and there may even be a little left over for me to put a deposit on a place of my own.'

She repeated the information she had gained, grunting at her son's quiet whistle.

'Wow! That's awesome.'

'We can only hope. Your father didn't hold back when it came to spending money—and borrowing every cent of it.'

He snorted. 'What's happening with Warren? Have the police caught up with him?'

'Oh yes. That was another revelation today. We popped into the police station too and the young constable said they'd tracked Warren down somewhere near Townsville. He's working on a mango farm now so we can't complain about his work ethics,' she said dryly. 'Anyway, they've questioned him and taken a statement. He still swears he wasn't near the shed when the accident happened and unless or until someone can prove he was, they can't charge him with anything. He told them that when he noticed the truck heading for home, he thought your father must have received a call to come to the house for something—or someone. So, Warren continued on the header, filling the field bin, and didn't come looking for Jack for what he estimates would have been around an hour. If Jack's hat hadn't been on the ground below the silo ladder, no one would have thought to check further. They found a torn piece of his shirt caught on a rivet beside the hatch.'

The reality of Jack's death flashed through Helen's mind and her blood ran cold. What would he have been thinking? Would he have realised his fall was one of no return? What would have happened if the silo hadn't been checked?

She could only hope it was quick.

'Do the police believe him—Warren, I mean?'

'I've no idea. I thought it was good of them to let me know where things are at though.'

'Fair enough. Hard to prove with no security cameras set up or anyone else around. Probably a good thing you weren't home, Mum.'

A sudden stab of guilt gripped her. 'I can't help thinking that if I'd been here, it wouldn't have happened.'

Steve breathed heavily but didn't answer.

It had appeared to be an unfortunate accident—one too horrendous to dwell on. Either Jack had slipped or was pushed into the grain silo. With the auger running and tonnes of grain already in the steel depths, when he fell he would have been sucked into the pit of sorghum in a flash.

'Forget about that now, Mum. I'll be down next week, and we'll get stuck into packing up, yeah?'

Helen's smile wobbled. *I'm so lucky to have you three. How did I let things get so bad?* 'That sounds great. Thanks, darling.'

4

____

*E*lizabeth Downs, May 2004 – Helen

Helen reached into the freezer for the peas and pressed the icy cold packet against her cheek bone.

It wasn't pain that caused the prickling behind her eyes. It was shock. Working in the yards with feisty cattle, drafting almost full-grown calves from their pregnant-again mothers was always fraught with danger. So keeping her wits about her and acting swiftly when a belligerent cow objected to her calf being sent into a different pen was important—potentially lifesaving.

But this was different. Despite Jack's mood swings, his often irrational criticism and dismissal of her, he had never hit her before—at least not deliberately.

When the blow had struck hard, she'd swivelled, stumbling but not quite falling. She'd looked up, expecting to have to leap over the yard rail to avoid an argumentative bovine. But instead, it had been Jack glowering at her. With her ears ringing and the bellow of cattle all around, she hadn't been able to make out his words but had a very good idea of what they were.

Uncertain of what she'd done wrong, she'd taken his dismissive flick of a hand as her chance to escape—and she had.

Slumping onto a kitchen chair, she leaned over the table, her head in her arms and her face resting on the icy package.

The shrill ring of the landline phone jolted her out of her misery. She stared at it while its persistent pitch continued, demanding attention.

Hoping it would stop before she reached it, she struggled to her feet and crossed the room, slowly lifting the handset. 'Hello?'

'Hi, Helen. It's Lucy. Have you got a minute to talk?'

'Sure.' The last thing she felt like was talking to anyone, but Lucy was her friend and despite her own harrowing few years, had remained positive and chirpy. Perhaps she was just what Helen needed to snap her out of her confusing cloud of depression.

'It was a year last week since Robert died,' Lucy said.

Helen's stomach clenched. Amidst her own traumas, she had completely forgotten the anniversary of her best friend's shocking situation—the day when not only her husband was killed in a small plane accident, but so was her father and their neighbour, the pilot.

'A tough week for both Adam and I, but school holidays start next week and Adam wants to stay with his cousins for a few nights. So ... I thought I might take a road trip and visit you?'

Suddenly alert, Helen cast her eyes around the room, resting on the shabby furniture. With the busy season of weaning cattle, shifting irrigation, and making hay before the first frost arrived, cleaning the house had been reduced to the bare minimum—a quick vacuum and mop of the floors when she could, and piling the mound of dirty clothing into the washing machine before she was summoned to help Jack again. So spiders persisted with their web construction in every corner and the previous week's dust storm that had coated the windows with a brown sheen was still evident.

But it wasn't only the house that sent an icy chill through her. It was what went on inside the homestead, especially when Jack was in a bad mood—and she could never judge when that would happen.

How can I let my friend see how we live? Tim has gone silent, won't talk to anyone. Although, according to Steve, his behaviour is normal when he's not here.

Tim was her firstborn—a sensitive child whose eyes grew wide and dark, his lip quivering, when raised voices or mute moodiness hung over the household. She tried hard not to but could never treat all her children the same. Steve had always been more reactive, prone to answering his father back and bracing for the backhander or punch on the arm when he did, then walking away with his head held high and a sneer on his face. Lisa was unlike either of her brothers. From birth, she had smiled—a happy, easy-going little girl who enjoyed life and adored her brothers and mother. If she'd ever formed a negative opinion about her father, no one knew—not even her own family. Would that change when she started high school the following year?

'Oh, Lucy. I'm so sorry. It's not a good time right now.' Her hand flew to her cheek. The bruising would be at its worst in another two days and having Lucy see her like that was unthinkable. 'We're really busy with weaning and making hay before winter arrives. Perhaps we could meet in another few weeks—in Emerald or somewhere else that suits you?'

Her thoughts raced. Although neither of her parents would visit the farm any more, they loved having the grandchildren visit. For a small town, their newsagency kept them busy, but the children were old enough to help out—not only in the business but also in their Papou's abundant vegetable garden, where his

Greek heritage and love of good food and gardening were beginning to rub off on them. Certain her parents were aware all was not well on Elizabeth Downs, Helen had never been able to discuss her fears with them. She was an only child and her children their only grandchildren. Family was everything to them. Her mother's frequently repeated words made her chest ache. "Children and family life are like gold. Never let them go."

And she never could, never would leave Jack—for her parents' sake.

Somehow, she would keep trying to change him. To encourage him to see the happiness in their lives and make him understand how his moodiness affected them all. But how she was going to do that, she had no idea.

The line had gone silent for a prolonged moment before Lucy answered. 'That sounds lovely, Helen. We'll do that. Meanwhile, you look after yourself and we'll catch up soon.'

'Thanks, Lucy. I'm sorry.'

They said goodbye and hung up, then Helen returned to the kitchen chair.

She understood Jack's lack of tolerance was largely due to recovering from the previous two years of drought. The increased costs of fodder and cattle purchases, the debts to aid that recovery were affecting everyone in the north. But to take it out on her and the children was not right—or fair.

Covering her face with her hands, Helen allowed the long-held hot tears of shame, sorrow, and desperation slide down her face.

5
____

2 *025 – Helen*

'Helen,' Lucy said when she called back hours later. 'I've been thinking. Once this is over—I mean the investigation and getting the farm ready for sale, would you like to come over here for a while? We've finished the new annexe and with summer about to begin, it will be a nice time to be in Scotland.'

Helen switched the handpiece to her other ear as she digested Lucy's offer. She'd never been to another country. She hadn't even explored Queensland, and the suggestion of visiting Tasmania or Western Australia had always been laughed at by Jack. *'Why do you want to go anywhere but here? This is where we belong—the best place in the world,'* he'd said. Her stomach did a flip as the thought of visiting one of her oldest friends on the other side of the earth flourished.

'That's really kind of you, Lucy. I don't know what to say—I-I mean I would love to but there is so much to deal with here, I can't think beyond securing a sale for this place.'

'Of course not. I understand. It's just a suggestion. Once you've dealt with all that's on your shoulders, you might feel like a change.'

The only change I'm likely to feel is freedom—and quite possibly, poverty!

Unwilling to share those details, Helen remained non-committal but allowed hope and a flutter of excitement to grow inside her. 'Thanks heaps, Lucy. I'll think about it. How was your lambing season?' Changing the subject was the best she could cope with and for the next ten minutes, she let her mind drift into Lucy's world as her friend chatted happily about the blissful spring they were having, the success of their increasing flock of Scottish Blackface sheep, and the excitement of the upcoming wedding of Fergus's nephew and his Australian fiancée, Ingrid.

By the time they ended the call, Helen's heart was thumping against her ribs. Would it be possible? Getting away from the property—and district—she had lived in for decades remained a dream. But now ...? Perhaps it wasn't out of the question. It needn't be for long and a holiday in a completely different environment with an old friend might be just what she needed while she thought about her future—and whatever that may hold. She had her own savings account that, if she was careful, might just allow her to visit Lucy on the Isle of Skye.

While her thoughts wavered, unanswered questions and years of heartbreak fought inside her. Practicality seesawed with possibility.

Then she drew a deep breath and shook her head, her heart aching with shattered hope.

Don't even think about it. You've got a farm to sell and a future to consider. Scotland is just a pipedream.

THE NEXT WEEK passed in a flurry. Helen and Lisa scrubbed every corner, washed windows, curtains, and trawled through photos before packing them into boxes and stowing them inside cupboards. They rearranged throws and cushions to cover the worn sofas—just in case Clint brought prospective buyers to look at the place—and when Tim arrived and stayed for two days, they drafted cattle for the next sale and sorted out the sheds.

Each morning, Helen baked a loaf of bread or a cake—her way of wrapping gratitude into something comforting for the family she cherished and providing a welcome for visitors.

There had been a lightness in the air. A feeling of euphoria. During their time together, all of them had talked, laughed, and cracked pathetic jokes as they worked, reminding Helen of how it should have been when they were growing up but never was if Jack was around.

A wave of helplessness had cloaked her as she and Lisa waved goodbye to Tim and Steve. Their childhood should have been better. Happier. And although none of them shed blame on her for their early years, her guilt still remained.

LISA WAS her usual positive self and hugged her mother before reluctantly getting into her car. It was her final morning before she had to return to the vet clinic and the sun was just peeping over the eastern horizon.

'I'll ring when I get to the flat,' she called to Helen.

'Drive safe, darling. And remember to stop every two hours for a break, even if it's only for ten minutes. If you get too tired, please find a motel room for the night.'

'Yes, Mum.' Lisa grinned. 'And you ring me the minute an offer is suggested.'

Helen returned her smile and nodded as Lisa hung her arm out the window and waved.

A sense of loss mingled with excitement filled Lisa as she drove away. She had loved her country upbringing. But as her father's erratic, violent behaviour had increased, life had changed, with happy times becoming filled with anxiety and fear. She'd hidden it well, but it had been a relief to finish school and move away. With the exception of missing her mother and brothers—and the horse her father had sold without whispering a word to her—there had been nothing to entice her home again.

She sighed and flicked the music volume up with her thumb. A twelve-hour drive to the Sunshine Coast was daunting but one she had made often enough to know she could reach the comfortable brick unit before dark, provided there were no major roadworks or hold-ups. Her friend and flatmate, Cassie, would be at work. Lisa hoped she'd leave something tasty in the fridge for her to heat up for dinner.

Her thoughts wandered to her mother's conversation with Lucy and then her. She contemplated the invitation Lucy had made. Scotland was somewhere she wanted to visit one day, and she was sure her mother would too once she had a chance to stop worrying about everything else. Her dearest wish was for the sale price of Elizabeth Downs to exceed the debt, surprising them all and allowing her mother to create a new life for herself. And if that new life could include a holiday in Scotland, then that would be totally amazing. Perhaps she would go too? She and her mother were best friends, and now her father was out of the picture, she was certain the real Helen would emerge—the one Lisa had always considered was being weighed down by her fierce belief in responsibilities and loyalty.

She smiled to herself and then, as the kilometres ticked by, she reduced the volume of her playlist and let her mind drift. Scotland. Or more to the point, the Isle of Skye. Ever since her mother had shared Lucy and Fergus's story, she had wanted to visit. She pictured the rugged hills, pretty, bush-clad valleys and white-painted houses dotted around the shores, exactly like those she'd seen in books and on television programs.

The idea sprang unexpectedly and her plans grew. By the time she'd covered another fifty kilometres, she had it mapped out. She would talk to her brothers and if they were in agreement, she'd extend her leave and urge their mother to take the break she deserved. The timing was perfect. It didn't matter if the farm wasn't sold. She was sure Shelley would be happy to feed the chooks and her husband could check on the stock— after all, her mother had done the same for them numerous times throughout the years.

Yep. I reckon when all this is over, Mum, you and I are off to Scotland.

6

———

*S*he was on the final leg of her journey, motoring down the M1 approaching her turn-off when her phone rang.

'Hello?'

'Hi there!' Tim's voice was high with excitement. 'I've had an idea and thought I'd run it past both you and Steve.'

He shared his suggestion and she laughed.

'You read my mind! I was literally thinking the same. A trip will give her time to process all that's happened, and she'll have a good friend to confide in. By the time she comes home, hopefully there'll be a contract on the farm. Then Mum will have a better idea of the next step she needs to take. Do you reckon Steve will be in on it?'

'I'm sure he will. And he and I can join forces to

pay Mum's airfare and a rental car.' He chuckled. 'I know vet nursing is not exactly a highly paid career.'

The exhaustion that had begun to creep through her disappeared in a flash. Her heart raced. 'Thanks, Tim. Shall I ring Steve or will you?'

'I will and ring you back. Take care on that road, hey? There's plenty of idiots about, even if you're not one of them.'

She spat out a choking laugh. 'Thanks for your confidence.'

'Just doing the big-brother thing.'

'Good on you. I will. Talk again soon.' She grinned as a burst of excitement shot through her. 'Bye, Tim. Love ya.'

'Love ya back.'

She switched her full attention to the increasing traffic around her and allowed the smile to spread across her face.

I'm going to ask for three weeks of leave—which is long overdue anyway.

For a moment, her heart plummeted. What if Stuart, her boss, said no? They were always busy at the practice. But ... they had just employed another two nurses, so perhaps it wouldn't be a problem? With renewed hope, thoughts began to swirl, and she hummed the Skye Boat song, tapping her steering wheel with rhythmic fingers.

ON THE FIRST OF MAY, with Elizabeth Downs in the capable hands of neighbours Bill and Shelley and the real estate agent, Clint, Helen and Lisa's flight took off from Brisbane. Feeling her mother's jittery foot against hers, Lisa squeezed Helen's fingers, holding them firmly until the plane was well into the heavens and levelling off. Her mother had never flown anywhere, least of all to the other side of the world, so her nervousness was to be expected. Once the seatbelt sign clicked off and the cabin crew began moving around, Lisa released her grip and shot Helen a smile.

'Shame we couldn't afford business class, but hey, we've got each other and will be fine. Shall we find a movie to watch?' Lisa touched the screen in front of Helen, directing her to scroll through the entertainment menu.

While she did the same, the butterflies in her own stomach began to settle. Drawing a deep breath, she reflected on the trip she and Cassie had taken almost two years earlier—their visit to Canada to attend the Calgary Stampede. It had been fun, the weather perfect, and she had adored the extra week they'd spent in the Rocky Mountains. As her first overseas trip, the long flight had been exciting and she hadn't thought about the discomfort of sitting in the same seat for hours on end. This time though, she was already tired from long days at the surgery. After which, she had driven to the farm, collected her mother, and returned to the coast, leaving Helen's car behind. They'd stayed one night in Lisa and Cassie's flat before catching the airport shuttle bus to Brisbane.

After selecting their chosen movies, Lisa pushed her seat back, tucked her neck-cushion around her, and relaxed.

AFTER WHAT FELT to Helen like more than a week than a twenty-four-hour period, they finally collected their little black rental car from Glasgow airport and began the journey to Mallaig.

'Remember our deal, Mum? I'll drive but you have to stay awake.'

Helen nodded, swallowing her tiredness and remaining silent about her aching back. She'd managed to snatch an hour or so of sleep on each of the sectors and was grateful for the two-hour break in Dubai where they could at least stretch their legs, clean their teeth, and generally attempt to straighten their tired limbs. But now, surrounded by gorgeous green countryside and with a brilliant blue sky above, the exhaustion melted away as intoxicating childish delight took over.

They reached the B and B Lisa had arranged in the

tiny village of Arrochar in the late afternoon, checked in, and made themselves a cup of coffee. Then they set off walking around the loch and village, enjoying the surprising warmth of the spring evening as they ambled along. An hour later, fatigue caught up with Helen and she stopped, pulling Lisa by the arm as she slumped onto a bench seat beside the path.

'Time to head back I think,' Lisa said, studying her mother. 'Shall we get a pizza at that pub?'

'Sounds lovely. I'm not really hungry. Just tired. But I suppose we'll sleep better with something in our stomachs.'

Lisa nodded and they rested in silence, their gazes fixed on the gentle lap of water against the pebbly shore. A few minutes later, Helen rested her hand on Lisa's.

'Let's do it. Pizza, shower, and bed.'

'Sounds like heaven!'

With her head still feeling like cottonwool but less tired than she'd been the previous evening, Helen woke early, surprised to check her watch and see it was only five o'clock. The sun was already high in the sky, and a gull screeched somewhere outside their room.

By the time she had showered and dressed, Lisa had made coffee for them both. While they waited for the breakfast room to open, they repacked their bags, loaded the car, and set off for another walk around the village. A feverish impatience to reach their destination and her old friend suddenly consumed Helen. The weather was perfect—totally unexpected sunshine bathing the village with its warmth. She dwelt on the contents of her suitcase—filled with winter layers, scarves, and jackets—and looked up at the sky.

'I think we should have brought lighter clothing?'

Lisa gave her a wry grin. 'Yeah. Maybe. Who knows though? We've been warned that we could experience all four seasons in one day—so we might be needing those thermal leggings by tonight.'

Helen laughed, her heart light with exhilaration. 'Come on. It's nearly seven. Let's have breakfast and get on the road. I can't wait to see Lucy.'

Three hours and six photo-stops later, they arrived in the small harbour town of Mallaig, almost an hour before they were due to board the ferry to the Isle of Skye. Helen paced up and down the wharf until Lisa hooked her arm into her mother's and marched her back into the village a few hundred metres away. There, she found a café and bought them both a cup of tea.

Eventually, they boarded the ferry, their little car tightly packed amongst dozens of others on the deck below them. They stood at the bow of the boat and watched Mallaig fade behind them as the tree-clad shores of the Isle of Skye grew clearer.

Forty minutes later, they drove off the Armadale pier and turned left at the sign indicating Ardvasar.

Helen opened her phone and read the instructions Lucy had sent her. 'We go past the hotel, up the hill, and continue toward the Aird of Sleat.'

While concentrating on her mother's directions, Lisa kept her eyes on the narrow road ahead, pulling into a passing bay for an oncoming vehicle as they reached the hilltop. As they descended the other side of the hill, breathtaking scenery spread out in front of them—lush green fields dotted with sheep, white painted cottages surrounded by colourful flowers, and pockets of bushes and trees overlooking a gentle sea.

'Wow. This is absolutely gorgeous!'

'Isn't it?' Helen pointed to a croft on the next hill, facing the water, and with a new extension on the white-painted stone cottage. 'I think that's it!'

She brightened as they drew closer, her weariness forgotten as they crawled slowly up the narrow lane. The slim, familiar figure of her dear friend raced to open the gate in front of them.

'Lucy!' Throwing the door open the second Lisa halted, Helen leapt out and the two friends fell into each other's arms, alternately laughing, hugging, and eventually stepping back to appraise each other.

'It's so good to see you again,' Lucy said.

Helen released a whoosh of breath and gazed into Lucy's green eyes, allowing a lifetime of pain, guilt, and loneliness to melt away.

Her chance for a new beginning had arrived. And, despite the cauldron of emotions swirling inside her, she was going to make the most of it.

7

____

Sprawled on the couch in the quaint Airbnb cottage, Dr Michael Blakeney closed the book and rested it on the coffee table. He lifted his gaze to the loch, his mind far from the gentle waves lapping the sandy shore.

He had been on the Isle of Skye for three days and the weather had been perfect. But now, with rain predicted for western Scotland in the coming week, he reconsidered his plans.

His gaze was drawn to the book again—*Walking with Wade* by George Reynolds. *Exploring General Wade's Lost and Forgotten Military Roads* wasn't his normal book of choice—he usually preferred to bury himself in a good crime novel. But it had caught his eye and he'd pulled it from the shelf of his accommodation and flicked through it, the author's introduction capturing him. Before he realised, he'd read a hundred pages.

Perhaps I could head east and hike a couple of the stretches around Aviemore while it's raining on this side of the country? The thought hovered while he made himself a cup of tea and repacked his rucksack for the following day.

It had been a hideous two years. He'd tried everything to forget. To bury his guilt. He'd cycled for kilometres every day until he was sideswiped by a truck and miraculously avoided serious injury. Then he'd switched to swimming before the weather got too cold and he found he didn't enjoy it any more. Finally, he'd begun hiking and, in particular, driving to the Blue Mountains at every opportunity where he could climb the steep tracks and fall into bed at night, too exhausted to think.

Walking had been good for both his health and mind and, when the catalyst had been falling asleep in the car park outside his workplace, he'd known it was time to take a break from the hustle and bustle of the huge Sydney hospital and fulfil a desire to climb some of the Scottish *Munros*—the challenging hills measuring more than three thousand feet in height. His research had revealed great climbing opportunities within the Cuillin Mountains of the Isle of Skye, so he'd decided to begin his outdoor pursuits there after reading, "The Munros draw many international hikers and mountaineers, providing a training ground for more adventurous plans like attempting the Himalayas or Andes". It seemed the changing weather and treacherous winds of the Scottish highlands were essential conditions in preparing for higher summits.

He wasn't training for anything special but still, he shuddered. Guilt plagued him every waking moment, pushing him as far away as possible from his shattered marriage and workplace. Then, after avoiding an accident while driving home, he'd accepted he needed a break. A week later, he'd boarded a flight to Scotland, convincing himself that hard physical exertion and isolation was exactly what he needed—then he'd slept all the way to Dubai.

His phone rang as he sat on the step in the mellow twilight, sipping his cup of tea. A smile spread across his face as a photo of his son appeared on the screen. 'Hi, mate. How're things?'

'Gidday, Dad. All good. I finish my locum on Friday and have nothing planned. Thought I'd come and join you.'

Michael blinked. It had been months since he'd seen Julian and despite their regular phone catch-ups, he didn't remember his son mentioning his stint in a rural New South Wales veterinary practice was coming to an end. Perhaps he'd missed it? Grimacing, he thought back to the previous couple of conversations. He'd been constantly tired, stressed, and out of sorts, so it was possible Julian had told him and he hadn't listened.

'Really? That would be great.'

'I'll jump online and book a flight. If I catch a train to Inverness, can you pick me up?'

'Of course. Let me know the details and I'll be there.'

'Great. I'll pack my hiking gear—and send you an update. Talk again soon.'

'Okay. Bye now.'

And with the conversation having lasted less than two minutes, Julian had disconnected.

Michael chuckled. The relationship between him and Julian had wavered precariously when Nita had left, but slowly, thankfully, their bond had cemented again. They shared a similar build—tall and athletic— and their love of outdoor pursuits had given them a mutual understanding of everything nature-related. Similarly, their desire to help and heal others was strong until Julian hinted he might follow his father down the medical path. It had been a particularly gruelling week of long working hours with obstruction from the medical hierarchy for Michael, so he'd suggested animal medicine as an alternative.

Veterinary work could be dirty and tiring but not having to wrestle with the failing health system, egotistical surgeons, or drug-affected, abusive patients, was a definite plus. So, after a long and revealing conversation with his son, Julian had thrown himself into schoolwork then university and after spending a few years in a city veterinary practice, was now enjoying a variety of short-term contracts in rural towns.

Michael's thoughts drifted to Amy, his beautiful, bright young daughter. Lowering his head into his hands, he tried but failed to wipe the guilt from his aching heart.

If only I had listened. If only you had stayed a little longer.

8

____

For three days after Helen and Lisa's arrival on Skye, the weather held, providing blissful, warm days filled with sunshine. After breakfast and the morning's chores each day, they'd explored the local area.

The following morning, the women joined Lucy and Fergus as they checked their sheep, releasing the confident ewes and lambs into the paddock and caring for those still in the maternity shed. With a picnic packed, once again the four of them set off to explore more of Skye.

'In another two weeks, you won't be able to find a car park in Portree—or at any of the special sites,' Fergus said dourly. 'The place will be heaving with tourists and those of us who live here year-round will have to postpone appointments until autumn.'

'You make it sound like tourism's a problem?' Helen frowned, a little stunned at Fergus's statement. 'I thought Scotland would welcome the boost in income?'

'It's not that tourism is unwelcome. It's the issue around the amount of traffic,' Lucy said.

'In what way?' Lisa asked.

Fergus drew a deep breath, gripping the steering wheel with white-knuckled hands, as if discussing the problem weighed heavily on his shoulders.

Helen had taken an instant liking to the big Scot. He had a gentle face and the bluest eyes she had ever seen, making it hard to avoid staring into them when he spoke.

'Following the pandemic lockdown, most Brits became cautious about leaving the country—which was fair enough,' Fergus said. 'So as soon as they could move around, many shelved their regular holidays to Spain or somewhere else in Europe and purchased motorhomes and camping gear and began exploring their own "backyard" instead. With the Skye bridge making access easy and affordable, we had thousands of people visit. They discovered what we've always known ... that Skye is a beautiful place to live and to holiday. That then led to those who could afford it buying property here. Cottages, sheds, hotels, and vacant crofts were snapped up and converted into holiday lets. You know, Airbnb's and stuff like that. And now the population skyrockets every summer.'

'And a lot own an annexe or something to rent out during summer for a much-needed extra income,' Lucy added with a chuckle. 'We've done the same—and now you two are able to stay without being crowded into our wee cottage.' She shot Helen and Lisa a warm smile. 'The problem is the infrastructure is still to catch up. As you can see, many of roads are single lane with passing bays. European and other visitors who are used to driving on the right-hand side of the road get confused and don't understand our rules.' As she spoke, an oncoming campervan halted in the middle of the road. Despite having a passing bay on their side, the driver seemed unable to understand what was required, subsequently blocking the road and clearly expecting Fergus to somehow provide a path on which they could continue their journey.

'Perfect example,' Fergus said with a wry grin, glancing in the rear-vision mirror and changing into reverse. 'Just as well there's no one behind us.' He shot backwards until he reached a passing bay fifty metres distant and on their side of the road, then beckoned the oncoming driver through.'

'I see what you mean,' Helen said, chuckling.

'That's not the biggest problem though,' Lucy said screwing up her nose. 'Because tourists are, at this point anyway, legally allowed to camp pretty much anywhere on the Isle, they do. That's okay—unless they're parked across your driveway or the paddock gate you want to put sheep in—but emptying their portable toilets onto the roadside vegetation is not.'

'Oh yuck!' Lisa snorted. 'And nobody stops them?'

'We don't have enough resources to police them and until laws change and facilities are installed, there's not much we can do.'

Helen sank back into the seat and shook her head. 'Gosh, I had no idea but I can see why the locals are worried.'

'Yes—although we can't complain,' Fergus added. 'Coachloads of tourists visit from Edinburgh and Glasgow and now the cruise ships come into Portree harbour, so the island's a lot wealthier than it was a decade or so ago. We just need more money spent on roads, designated camp sites, and public parking—like all the pretty places in the UK.' He grinned in the rear-vision mirror and swung left onto an even narrower road. 'Luckily some of us know all the best places to take our visitors.'

Helen returned his smile. She was delighted to witness the adoration he and Lucy had for each other. They walked hand-in-hand at every opportunity, his broad bulk dwarfing Lucy's slender figure as they exchanged understanding and caring glances, their love seemingly encompassing those around them.

Helen couldn't remember the last time she and Jack had held hands.

Probably walking down the aisle after we were married.

A sudden pain stabbed her insides—so intense she glanced down but saw no wound. Was it envy? She stared out the window, barely registering the colourful wildflowers along the roadside or the lush green paddocks flowing down to the shore. In her mind, she saw only dust, miserable stock and a disgruntled man shouting angrily at a dog. Her husband, Jack. When hers and Lucy's marriages were new and life was chaotic with young children, feeding workers, and coping with the never-ending round of chores, their phone conversations had been filled with interruptions but were bright and chatty. But as the decades had passed, they became short and infrequent—particularly following the never-forgotten phone call from Lucy the year after Robert had died.

Straightening her shoulders, she reached over and squeezed her daughter's hand, switching her thoughts to the present and dismissing her past with a tiny head shake. 'How lucky are we to have such fabulous weather?'

'We've done well,' Lisa said, flicking her forefinger in the air as she ticked off the places of interest they'd investigated before arriving in Scotland. 'Dunvegan Castle, a thorough tour of the MacRae estate.' She paused as both Lucy and Helen laughed and Fergus emitted a half-chuckle. 'Not to mention the Armadale gardens and castle ruins, two distilleries, and now we're about to explore Elgol Beach, Spar Cave, and then the ancient St Colombus cemetery.'

'I think tomorrow we'd better do one of the walks we said we'd hike while we're here,' Helen said. 'What do you recommend, Lucy?'

Lucy grimaced. 'If it's another nice day, I recommend you get an early start and head to the Quiraing Walk. It's likely to be busy all summer but both that and the Old Man of Storr should be okay for another couple of weeks. I'm sorry but you'll be on your own though as Fergus and I need to visit the accountant and do some shopping.'

'Here we are,' Fergus announced and before either Helen or Lisa could answer, they'd pulled into a parking area facing the sea. 'Time to enjoy a different Skye coastline. A bit rocky but a good spot to look at the Cuillins. There's lots of photo opportunities and nice walks around here.'

Between them, they hauled the picnic basket, flasks, and hats from the boot and headed to a sheltered part of the beach.

'Isn't that mountain range amazing, Mum?'

With her back nestled against a comfortable rock, Helen glanced up at her daughter before fixing her gaze on the dark, foreboding cliffs of the Cuillin Mountains on the other side of the water. The little she'd read about them had indicated they were one of the most challenging mountain ranges in the UK and a popular destination for experienced mountaineers. A shiver ran through her as she studied the jagged peaks. She imagined ancient tales emanating from them. Historical accidents and worse.

'Tea?' Lucy asked.

Helen beamed at her, swinging her gaze from the moody mountains to the steaming mug Lucy held. 'Yes please.'

'They look a bit adventurous for us, but we might do as Lucy suggests ... leave early and head north. Maybe hike the Quiraing Walk tomorrow?' Lisa said.

Helen blew out a relieved breath that hiking the black cliff tracks across the harbour had been dismissed. She was fit and enjoyed walking but attempting the challenging and seemingly inhospitable range—from where she sat anyway—held no appeal. 'Sure. I've been waking at five anyway so we might as well beat the crowd.'

She couldn't put her finger on it, but something deep inside her suggested extra care was needed when hiking in Scotland. Perhaps it was the changeable weather? Although she considered herself an adventurous spirit, she was not a risk-taker. That title had been Jack's.

Perhaps that's what happened? He stepped too close to

check how full the silo was, or perhaps he was watching the flow and forgot how slippery standing on a silo could be.

Swallowing the chilling thought, she took a mouthful of tea and reached for a sandwich. Climbing gentle tracks was not something that would deter her.

9

It was barely eight o'clock when Michael parked the rental car in the designated parking lot. Opposite the car park, the rugged range stretched into the hills, the track options clearly displayed on numerous signs.

Michael hitched his rucksack onto his back and lifted his gaze. The predicted rain was nowhere to be seen, the blue sky clear and the gentle breeze cool.

His smile grew as he strode along the undulating section of the track, his thoughts dwelling on the previous evening's conversations with his enthusiastic son. Julian had called a second time within an hour, excitedly announcing his flights and train trip were booked. He would meet his father at the railway station in Inverness in four days' time.

While he waited for both his son and the predicted

weather change, Michael had made the decision to explore the easier walks on Skye—the ones he could enjoy without mishap and increase his fitness while saving the more challenging walks to share with Julian. Today would be the perfect start.

His long legs covered the well-formed path at a cracking pace, taking the increasing elevation in his stride.

A little after nine-thirty, he reached the summit, slumped onto a rock, and pulled his flask from his rucksack. A strong breeze wound its way around the rocks, but Michael barely noticed it. The scenery in every direction was more than he could have ever imagined and he revelled in the freedom. The frantic Sydney emergency department threatened to invade his thoughts, but he pushed it away, instead breathing deeply and imagining what life must have been like in these harsh conditions a hundred years earlier.

Back down the track, dots grew into fellow hikers, and as the first group drew close, bursts of breathless conversation drifted on the breeze. He finished his cup of tea, stashed the flask in his rucksack, and prepared to begin his descent as the group of walkers approached—a couple and two children he guessed to be late primary-school age.

'Good morning,' he greeted them while standing to the side of the track to allow them to pass.

'Good morning,' they replied in heavy accents and nodded.

More people were now enjoying the trail as much as he was, the numbers significantly increasing with every bend.

He estimated he was halfway down when he approached two women sitting on the topside bank. An older, dark-haired one around his own age and the other—her tawny-coloured ponytail blowing in the wind—young, around Julian's age, he estimated. *Mother and daughter?* A quiver of alarm sliced through him. The woman's ghostly face turned to him as she leaned heavily on her young companion.

'Hello there. Are you alright?' he asked as he looked down on them.

'Mum slipped coming up that last little pinch. The rocks and track are wet from the waterfall, and she put out her hand to steady herself. And ...' Her voice shook. 'I think she might have broken her wrist.'

He slid his pack off and knelt in front of them. 'My name's Michael. May I have a look?'

'I think we need a doctor,' the girl said.

He stared at her for a second. 'I'm a doctor and am happy to help if you'd like me to?'

'Thank you,' the older woman whispered. 'I'm so silly. Just missed my footing and went down like a baby elephant.'

'I'm Lisa,' the younger woman said. 'And this is Helen, my mum.'

Michael smiled at Helen's attempt at humour. Even without a thorough examination, it was clear the wrist was broken.

Thank goodness it's not a compound fracture.

'Have you given your mum anything?' Michael met Lisa's eyes. 'Pain relief?'

She shook her head. 'No. It only happened a few minutes ago. I just helped her to sit here. I thought she was going to faint.'

Nodding, he whipped out a first-aid kit from his pack and punched two tablets into his palm. 'Can you swallow these—paracetamol? Best we do something about the pain before I take a more thorough look.'

Helen accepted them silently with her good hand and swallowed, reaching for the water bottle Lisa held out and washing them down.

'I've got a sling here and a magazine we can roll up and use as a splint.' Michael spoke reassuringly. While escaping the medical world had been one of his goals when planning this trip, there was no way he would walk past an injured person without providing some form of aid. 'Where are you from?'

'Australia,' Lisa said. 'Queensland.'

He smiled. 'I'm from New South Wales. Lucky hey? At least we speak the same language.'

Lisa chuckled, while the hint of a smile flashed across Helen's face.

For the next ten minutes, they talked quietly, thanking each of the passing walkers who also stopped and offered help.

After removing the phone from his pocket, Michael did a quick search of the local hospitals, establishing that although the Portree was closer, it was Broadford hospital that had the resources and equipment needed for orthopaedic surgery. They would have to drive there—another half hour from Portree.

'Okay. How's the pain now?' he asked.

While Helen's face was still pale, her eyes appeared clearer, the dullness of agony reduced. 'A bit better,' she said softly.

He smiled at her and reached out, probing her soft flesh with practiced fingers, his gaze flicking between her wrist and her expression. Helen's complexion was lightly tanned, her thick hair contrasting with her daughter's long, fine strands. Her eyes caught his. A rich brown—the colour of polished chestnuts.

'Well, there's no doubt you've got a nasty fracture there. We'll splint your arm with this magazine and immobilise it in a sling. Once you're feeling up to it, I think it best we head back to the car park. Okay with you?' He swung his gaze between the women, accepting Helen's nod as a yes.

'I've got phone reception,' Lisa said. 'I'll give Lucy a ring and ask her where we should take Mum.'

Michael raised his eyebrows. 'Lucy?'

'My friend,' Helen said. 'We're staying with her at the Aird of Sleat.'

'Perfect. I've checked the hospitals here and understand Portree doesn't have all the facilities we'll need. This is a popular place for hiking and no doubt yours won't be the first incident they've seen lately, but it might be better if we continue straight through to Broadford.' Michael smiled again while gently applying a bandage around the magazine and Helen's wrist. Then he raised the bound limb to rest against her collarbone and tied the sling firmly in place.

At Helen's whoosh of breath, he paused and their eyes met.

'Better?'

She nodded. 'Much.'

'Good. Lisa, do you think you could manage your mum's pack as well as yours? I'll walk beside her, and we'll stop whenever she needs a break. It's more than an hour back to the car park, but I presume you have a vehicle down there somewhere?'

'Yes.'

'Great. I'm going to call the hospital to let them know we're coming.'

Lisa nodded, and Helen shot him a weak smile.

As they set off, Michael walked closely enough to

assist if she became dizzy while distant enough to avoid invading her space. He caught a whiff of her perfume—a soft herbal fragrance that bore a hint of wildflowers. Pleasant and natural—with none of the overpowering headiness his ex-wife had insisted was her favourite.

Lisa scrambled ahead of them, turning at regular intervals to study her mother's face.

They stopped frequently, allowing Helen to rest and for Michael to readjust the sling. In his head, Michael calculated the distance between the car park and Broadford.

As though reading his mind, Helen asked, 'How long will it take to get to the hospital?'

He drew a breath and grimaced. 'About an hour and a half. We'll head straight there. No café stops on the way.'

Helen's grateful expression penetrated Michael's core, and his heart went out to her. Despite having treated hundreds of similar injuries in Australia, there was something about helping a patient in the mountains of Scotland that made the situation less stressful for him.

He felt appreciated—and he needed that.

10

___

*H*elen leaned her pounding head against the window. Her wrist throbbed. Michael's vehicle was in front of them, and Lisa's gaze alternated between her mother and the oncoming traffic.

'I'm okay, love. Just keep your eyes on that car—and the road.'

Closing her eyes, Helen practiced deep breathing and dreamed of the small cottage she hoped to buy. Somewhere in a rural Queensland town not too far from Lisa—somewhere neither too big nor too small with room to grow flowers and herbs. Her initial shock had eased, and slowly, incredulity crept in as her thoughts roved to Michael.

How lucky to have had not only a competent first-aider come to her rescue, but an experienced

Australian doctor. Was he really a doctor? He certainly seemed to know what he was doing, so she dearly hoped so.

Just be grateful doctors get time off for holidays—even if it means they have to help the walking wounded when they least expect it.

The hour after arriving at the hospital passed in a whirl. Forms were completed, examinations made, and X-rays taken—the results to be shared after being reviewed by an orthopaedic surgeon. While Helen rested on a temporary hospital bed with her daughter sitting on one side of her, Michael sat on the other, his handsome face creased in a frown, his jaw shadowed by a day or two's growth.

'You don't have to stay,' Helen said, hesitatingly. As her rescuer, dismissing him sent another shot of guilt through her. She secretly hoped he would stay a little longer, even if only to confirm his diagnosis.

They all looked up as Lucy burst through the door, her shoes tapping on the linoleum floor.

She bent and kissed Helen's cheek. 'You poor thing. Not such a fabulous walk after all?'

'The first part was gorgeous,' Helen said softly with a wry smile. 'It was coming back that wasn't so good.'

'Well, don't worry now. Fergus and I are here for you and once they've got you comfortable, I promise I'll look after you better—and that means you won't be doing any more hikes without me!'

They all laughed and Lucy turned to Michael, holding out her hand. 'Hello there. I'm Lucy. You must be the knight in shining armour Lisa mentioned?'

'I don't know about that.' Michael grinned. 'It certainly added more to my day than a solitary walk though.'

'I'm sorry about that,' Helen said, her forehead creasing. 'Perhaps I could buy you a coffee?'

'Don't feel obliged.' He stood up and pointed to Helen's wrist. 'I'd like to hear how you get on though. If I give you my number, would you mind flicking me a message?'

'Of course.' She smiled as her stomach spun. Was that due to pain—or something else totally unfamiliar?

After exchanging details, he said goodbye and left the room.

Helen and Lucy stared at each other for a moment. 'I approve of your rescuer,' Lucy chuckled.

Lisa rolled her eyes. 'I'm not sure the circumstances were the best—but things could have been worse. And a dishy doctor is never someone I would turn away.'

Before they had time to say more, a middle-aged man arrived, his neatly trimmed white beard perfectly matching his medical coat. 'I'm Hamish Donald,' he said. 'Attending doctor. Looks like you've had a busy morning.'

Helen smiled. 'Yes. Not quite what we'd planned.'

'Oh well. These things happen—despite our best intentions.' He paused and consulted the iPad in his hand. 'Looks like a clean break involving the radius. We'll try to get it lined up properly and plaster it. With the break close to the end of the bone, it can sometimes be a little tricky ... but we'll see how we go.'

Helen gulped. 'Okay.'

'Don't worry.' He put a reassuring hand on her shoulder. 'There are alternatives, but this is the quickest way to solve the problem and allow healing to begin.'

Half an hour later, the doctor's eyes met hers.

'We've tried to traction it, but it hasn't remained where we want it. Our option is to operate and insert a plate and pins but unfortunately our orthopaedic surgeon is away until the day after tomorrow. We can make you comfortable until then but if you'd rather not wait, we can send you to Inverness.'

'What do you recommend?'

He smiled. 'It's your call. But you're in good hands here and another couple of hours' travel may be a challenge you'd rather avoid.'

Her insides heaved at the thought of having to sit in a car for that long, especially as—if Inverness was anything like the busy city hospitals in Australia—she may have to wait for treatment when she got there. 'I'll do what you suggest. Will I have to stay here until them?'

'Not at this stage. We'll get you comfortable and you can go home.' He glanced at Lucy and Lisa. 'I'm assuming these two lovely ladies will be looking after you?'

'Yes. Helen and Lisa are staying with us,' Lucy said.

'Very good. Let's get you sorted. I'll send you home with painkillers. Don't be afraid to use them as prescribed.'

FOR THE NEXT HALF HOUR, Helen lay drowsily, feeling more fragile than she had in years.

'You okay, Mum?' Lisa held out a glass of water. 'Thirsty?'

She nodded and directed the straw into her mouth, swallowing a much-appreciated drink as she stared at the clunky support splint encasing her lower arm and hand.

A surge of warmth filled Helen's chest, rising slowly toward her face as she recalled the morning's events. She rested a hand on her throat, willing the heat to subside as the vision of Michael's gentle face entered her mind. He had simply been a doctor tending a patient. But something about him triggered a long-forgotten emotion. Was it kinship? Or was it some sort of physical attraction that was so foreign to her she couldn't recognise it?

She cleared her throat, admonishing herself. *It's the painkillers.*

A chance meeting on a busy hiking track only weeks after she'd buried her husband didn't shout romance. It spoke of kindness and professionalism— nothing more. Even if it circumstances had been differ- ent, if it had been months or years since Jack's death and she was lonely, to consider inviting another man into her life filled her with alarm. She'd been lonely ever since her kids left home and had become used to it.

And if I was looking for a companion, it would be my luck to find someone nice then discover he's happily married or totally disinterested.

Nevertheless, she seemed unable to stem the tide of gratitude. Dr Michael Blakeney certainly bore no resemblance to the family's aging GP back in Queens- land, or her deceased husband. Nor did he behave like any sort of knight, with or without shining armour. He was simply a person with skills to assist a middle-aged woman who'd stupidly slipped on a wet rock when she should have been paying more attention.

A smile quivered on her lips as she recalled her mother falling in love with one of the doctors in her final weeks of life. "Dementia" the doctor had said when her mum voiced her emotions in front of Helen.

Michael's appearance on the rocky hillside had been fortunate though—and, for someone she judged to be of a similar age to her own fifty-eight-almost-fifty-nine years, he was darn good looking.

'Mum. Are you listening?'

Helen started at Lisa's worried face. 'Sorry, love. Feeling a bit dopey, that's all.'

'Yeah well, I can't imagine why.' Her sarcastic comment was delivered with a grin. 'The nurse should be here any minute with your medication. Then we're heading home to Lucy's.'

'Thank you,' Helen whispered. It felt strange to be fussed over. But despite the hospitalisation event and the unfamiliarity of her circumstances, Helen relaxed into the soft pillows behind her head.

Strange, but so, so blissful!

11

————

 ack in the cottage overlooking the loch, Michael made himself a mug of coffee, picked up *Walking with Wade*, and slumped into the squishy couch.

The morning's events had rattled him. Not in a disappointing way but in a way he struggled to understand. Had he left Australia to get away from his work? It didn't seem so. The minute he'd encountered Helen and Lisa, assisting them had been automatic. He would have helped anyone and not for one second had he felt a reluctance in becoming involved.

Probably just habit—and everything I signed up for.

But ... he flicked through the pages of the book, unseeing as he relived the day's actions. Was the reason for coming to Scotland deep-seated? Something to do with what had happened two years earlier?

Or because he was lonely—not because his wife of more than thirty years had left him, but because he'd suddenly realised his work, often traumatic and almost always all-consuming, had used up every thread of emotion he had in his body? He had been working robotically, getting through the shifts as best he could, always achieving goals but being asked to give more.

He sipped his coffee, the emptiness inside him growing, fermenting like milk left in the sun. His turbulent mind reflected on the previous decade. There was no doubt the health department was struggling in New South Wales as funding was reduced and the population grew. They were not alone though. The story was the same throughout Australia and other countries around the world. He had tried so hard to fulfil the expectations of the powers-that-be and his patients. Had he failed? It certainly felt that way. Although fit and healthy, mentally he was spent.

The bleating of sheep jarred him from his gloomy depths, and he stood and walked to the open window as a flock of blackface sheep trotted past his cabin, a frantic border collie switching back and forth behind them and a casually-dressed man of around Julian's age strolling behind.

He looked up and met Michael's gaze, gave a wave, and called, 'Lovely evening!'

'Yes. It is.' Surprise consumed Michael for a long minute as he scanned his surroundings. The young man was right. It was a beautiful evening. The late sun shimmered on the loch and bees continued to buzz in the wildflowers surrounding the cottage.

Stepping outside, he smiled as the flock turned through a gate at the end of the lane, disappeared behind bushes, then reappeared and frisked into a fresh paddock.

If only life was that simple.

Helen's image rose in his mind, unexpected and vivid. Even through her pain, the warmth of her grateful smile was memorable. They'd shared little beyond the necessities of doctor and patient, yet in her gentle brown eyes he'd seen a sadness that spoke of something buried deep—something far more painful than a fractured wrist.

With a steadying breath, he turned and went inside. He understood all too well. He had his own secrets to keep.

Throughout his medical career he had treated every type of human patient. The dramatic, the violent, the complainers, the stoic, the too-sick-to-speak and occasionally, the perfect patient. One who, despite their pain, remained positive and exuded thanks.

In the short time he had spent with Helen, he was certain she was both stoic and positive. It would take more than a hiking accident to bring her down.

Shame I'll never see her again.

12

Helen was on the couch reading when Lucy arrived.

'Don't get up.' Lucy went straight to the kitchenette and filled the electric jug. 'Lisa's gone with Ingrid and the men. They're taking a flock of ewes and lambs to the common and I've done my essential jobs. So ... now it's just you and me, we can talk.'

Helen closed her book and placed it on the coffee table, tentative but relieved that this moment had finally arrived.

'Oh.'

Lucy warmed the teapot and set out mugs and a plate of biscuits on the tray. Helen had already shared how unhappy hers and Jack's marriage had been but was reluctant to say too much in case her friend thought she was weak and pathetic—too timid to fight back or leave. She wouldn't blame her. There had been plenty of times she'd felt that way herself.

Lucy placed the tray on the coffee table and handed a mug to Helen before slumping into the armchair opposite. 'It's time for sharing—and I mean everything!' Lucy said. 'Start at the beginning. We've got all morning.'

Before Helen had a chance to utter a word, Lucy held a hand up in a stop sign.

'In case I forget to tell you, I've invited Callum and Ingrid for dinner tonight. I'm sorry you haven't had a chance to get to know them before now—but it has been a kind of busy couple of days, hasn't it? They're such an important part of my family and I'm dying for you to meet them. Anyway, now it's your turn and I promise I won't interrupt again. Go for it.'

Helen swung her legs to the floor, sat up straight, and took a sip of her tea. Her voice quavered as she began. 'I can't tell you how often I wanted to share what was really going on—but every time ... I don't know. I guess I didn't have the courage.'

'I know.'

Drawing a deep breath, Helen forced her mind back to the early years, attempting to pinpoint when things had begun to go wrong.

'I think red flags started flying once all the children were at school. Maybe things had never been quite right and I'd been too busy to notice. But whatever it was, I had time to spend more time dealing with the bigger jobs on the farm—branding and tagging cattle, long hours driving the tractor during planting and harvesting. You know the drill. There are always so many jobs that are easier with two pairs of hands.' She took another mouthful of tea. 'Anyway, it gave Jack and I more time together—which should have been wonderful. Only it wasn't. Character traits I'd either never noticed or he'd kept hidden for years sprang up.'

Lucy raised her eyebrows as Helen continued, slowly unravelling the concerning events that had followed. Jack's criticism that progressed to a back-handed slap whenever she did something he wasn't happy with, the silent moods that continued for hours or even days, and the constant putdowns.

'I really thought it was me. He had me totally convinced I was useless—and I believed him. Looking back, I should have talked to our doctor earlier. It was he who made me realise it wasn't my fault. Maybe I should have left but I couldn't while Mum and Dad were alive. I kept hoping things would change—one day. Then once my parents were gone, times improved on the farm and I really imagined he would too.'

As Lucy gently encouraged more, tears ran unchecked down Helen's face while she revealed the life she'd led and the fears she'd hidden.

Their tea went cold as she described the day of

Jack's accident and the eventual news that his body had been found in the grain silo.

'It was such a relief, and I couldn't speak—just cried. The police thought I was distraught with grief.' She huffed and shook her head slowly. 'No one had any idea they were tears of shame, relief, and joyful liberation.'

Lucy leapt to her feet and sat beside Helen, gathering her friend in her arms. 'Oh, you poor darling. And all this time, you never told anyone?'

'My neighbour and friend, Shelley, had a fair idea. Her husband, Bill, sometimes gave Jack a hand and I'm sure he saw things he wasn't happy about but felt it wasn't his business to interfere. There was also gossip around town about Jack's infidelities.' She said the word cautiously, the hint of a smile touching her face. 'As you know, I worked a couple of nights a week and always kept in the kitchen, so patrons rarely saw me— but I still heard plenty I wasn't supposed to.'

'You're free now. You can move on and hold your head high. I don't know how you've done it ... but you were always the tough one of our little trio.'

They both laughed, quietly at first. Then, as the years of stress, worry, and terror slid from Helen's shoulders, her laugh deepened until both women had tears once again pouring down their faces. Only this time, they were tears of happiness.

Lucy stood and crossed the room to the kitchenette

again. 'I think another cuppa is needed.' She paused and turned to face Helen. 'Actually, you know what? I think we need something stronger. Hang on a tick. I'll be back.' She dashed out the door.

Her head dizzy with liberty, Helen stared through the window as Lucy hurried along the roofed pathway adjoining the main house and annexe.

She straightened the sling, surprised that even the dull pain that had plagued her through the night had eased. A sudden rush of guilt flashed through her. She hadn't thanked Michael properly—at least she didn't remember if she had. Shaking her head, she grunted softly.

What am I thinking? A chance meeting with another Australian—that's it. He probably hasn't spared me a thought and anyway, we'll never see each other again.

Lucy burst through the door with a bottle of sparkling wine in her hand.

She poured them each a glass and as they sipped, an unfamiliar sense of peace enveloped Helen.

Her phone rang as she placed the empty glass on the table. Glancing at it, she met Lucy's raised eyebrows. 'It's Michael,' she whispered as she tapped the green icon, her thoughts of seconds earlier pumping through her veins. 'Hello there.'

Lucy topped up their glasses but made no effort to leave as Helen answered the standard questions. Yes, she was fine. No, she hadn't done much except go for a gentle walk around the garden and to visit the lambing shed a couple of times. She looked up as Lucy flapped a hand in her face.

'Just a second, Michael. Lucy's trying to say something.'

'Put him on speaker,' Lucy commanded.

Helen did and Lucy spoke. 'Hi Michael. Are you doing anything tonight?'

A few silent seconds passed before Michael's warm voice responded. 'Nothing special. Why?'

'Why don't you join us for dinner?' Lucy said. 'Callum, Fergus's nephew, and his fiancée are coming, and it would be lovely to see you again and for you to meet them. They're both keen hikers so you'll have plenty in common.'

Helen's pulse thumped so hard she pressed her good hand against her chest.

'I'd love to. Thank you.'

They shared location details and ended the call.

'Right,' Lucy said as she reached out a hand and took Helen's. 'Come with me, my dear. We've got dinner to prepare and while you might not be able to do much chopping, you can stir and hand out advice.'

Helen chuckled as the final cloak of hopelessness slid away.

She might be pushing sixty, but she wasn't dead yet —and the future was looking brighter with every minute.

13

Laughter surrounded the table later that night. Callum and Ingrid were vivacious and welcoming, and Lucy had exceeded all expectations with a feast of roast lamb, vegetables, and a magnificent cheesecake for dessert.

Within an hour of everyone arriving, Ingrid had arranged to take Lisa on a "locals" tour of Portree the following day while Lucy took Helen back to hospital to have her wrist plated and pinned.

Michael felt a pang of regret as he turned down Fergus's invitation to join him and his friend, Ken, on a boat trip into the Sound. The plan was to do some fishing and then call in to Ken's holiday cabin on the Isle of Rum where they would cook the fish over an outdoor fire and enjoy the picnic Lucy and Fergus would prepare.

'I would have loved to join you,' Michael said with genuine disappointment. 'But my son is arriving in Inverness tomorrow and I've arranged to collect him then head to Aviemore for a couple of days.'

He caught Helen's intrigued look and grinned before clearing his throat. 'We're hiking a small portion of the historic roads General Wade was responsible for back in 1724. I've been reading a book about it and contacted the author.'

'Interesting,' Fergus said.

'Really?' Ingrid's eyes widened. 'Tell us more.'

Michael explained how the book had piqued his interest, so he had connected with the author online. 'By coincidence, he has a free day so offered to spend it walking with us. Being familiar with the tracks, he regularly repeats sections of walks. So ... Julian and I jumped at the chance.'

'That's wonderful,' Helen said hesitantly. 'Is your wife also joining you?'

He shook his head. 'My wife and I divorced some time ago.'

'I'm sorry.' Helen's eyes met his, filled with genuine understanding. 'Will you be coming back to Skye—after Aviemore I mean?'

'Yes. I've booked the Teangue cottage for a month so even if we spend a couple of nights elsewhere, it's my base.' A leap of delight shot through him as Helen's smile met his.

The conversation morphed to the predicted wild weather that was to hit the Hebrides, including Skye, Helen's surgery, and Lisa's list of still-to-visit places.

'It's a shame we won't have time to visit the Orkneys this trip,' Lisa said. 'There's so many things I'd love to see there.'

Michael caught Helen's pained expression before she touched her broken wrist with her good hand. His heart went out to her. *Don't feel guilty. It could easily have been Lisa nursing an injury.*

'Next time,' Ingrid replied. 'You'll all have to come back for our wedding.'

'Oh goodness,' Lisa laughed. 'You hardly know us. Won't you have enough guests with your families and friends?'

'My family's very small and it will be quite a casual affair so plenty of room for everyone.'

Michael blinked at the invitation. Within minutes of his arrival earlier that evening, he'd learned Ingrid was a nurse in the Broadford Hospital and before he knew it, she'd wheedled from him as much about his profession as he was prepared to share. About his personal life, he'd said nothing until Helen asked about his wife joining them—an issue he was surprisingly pleased to have cleared up.

'And we've only just met,' Michael stammered. 'You don't think it's early days for an invitation of that magnitude?'

'Of course not,' Ingrid chuckled. 'Whether you like it or not, your demonstration of being a good Samaritan in helping Helen automatically grants you entry to the MacRae friendship group.'

'Well ... that's about the most generous invitation I've received from someone not under the influence of drugs or alcohol.'

Callum roared with laughter. 'I suppose working in hospitals you'd see a lot we don't even think about.'

Michael grinned. *If only you knew. Best you don't.*

It was almost eleven o'clock before Callum and Ingrid said goodbye and everyone traipsed outside to their cars.

'I'd better be going too,' Michael said reluctantly. He couldn't remember having had such a pleasant, relaxing evening in years and was delighted when Fergus grasped his hand and shook it enthusiastically.

'When you get back to Skye, bring your son to see us. I'd love to talk more and perhaps we could convince Ken another fishing trip and a run over to Rum would be in order.'

Fergus stepped back, wrapping an arm around Lucy. They shared a long, loving look that wrapped Michael in an unexpected haze of envy.

Had it been the generous nips of whisky that had loosened Fergus's initially shy demeanour or was he always this gregarious? Michael grinned. There was a story here that he would love to know more about.

They nodded at each other before Michael was enveloped in Lucy's farewell embrace.

He exchanged a quick hug with Lisa then faced Helen, reaching for her hand and holding it as he leaned forward and touched her cheek with his lips. 'Don't worry about tomorrow. I've every confidence you'll feel much better after the surgery. Your wrist will heal quickly. When you get back, would you let me know how everything went? Please?'

Helen's smile wobbled for a second. 'Of course.'

Minutes later, he arrived at the cottage, the light finally fading under the early summer sun. His belly was full and so was his heart. He liked the gentle Scottish giant and Helen's bubbly friend, and despite looking forward to seeing Julian the following day, a surprised reluctance to leave this isle overwhelmed him.

He sighed and entered the dwelling, drew the curtains, and switched on the light.

When I get back to Australia, I will make changes. And the first will be to get out of Sydney and search for somewhere new to live. Hopefully somewhere as welcoming as here.

'OH! A MENU?' The last time Helen had been admitted to a hospital bed had been thirty years earlier, when her final baby—the one now standing in front of her—had been born. She had no recollection of being offered a menu on that occasion.

'You can have roast chicken and vegetables, mushroom and tomato pasta, venison casserole, or Cullen Skink. What the hell is Cullen Skink?' Lisa asked.

'I've no idea, love. It sounds revolting.' She screwed up her nose as the nurse entered the room.

The woman's glance flicked from her patient to Lisa. 'What sounds revolting?' Her voice was soft, her manner helpful.

'Cullen Skink.'

She laughed, shaking her head. 'It may not sound very nice but it's really delicious. Basically, it's leak and potato soup made extra thick and tasty with the addition of smoked fish and cream. Easy to digest and if you like seafood, something you might enjoy.'

'Oh. Okay.' Helen smiled at Lisa, remorse nipping at her at the knowledge she'd been so dismissive of a popular local dish. 'Tick that one please?'

'And for dessert? Apple crumble or fruit and ice-cream.' Lisa raised her eyebrows. 'I think I might stay and have dinner here.'

The nurse smiled indulgently. 'We do like to look after our patients.'

Helen grinned, 'Apple crumble please.'

'Right. Now that's sorted,' the nurse said. 'Let's

check you over and get ready for theatre. The doctor will be in shortly.'

HOURS LATER, Helen looked down at her wrist. It had been a long day, beginning with the early morning drive to the hospital before waving goodbye to Lisa and Ingrid.

'We'll be back to see you this afternoon when it's all over,' Lisa had said as she'd kissed her mother goodbye.

And now, despite the sun still being high in the sky, the nurse had informed her it was five-thirty and her dinner would be served shortly.

Rapid steps along the linoleum outside the room announced Lisa's arrival before her bright smile greeted Helen.

'Hi there,' she said softly. 'I popped in earlier but you were fast asleep, so Ingrid and I went to a café.'

'Where's Ingrid now?'

'She's catching up with one of the nurses—a friend. She works here remember? I wanted to see how you were before we head back to Lucy's though. So ... how are you?'

'I'm fine,' Helen said. 'Still under the influence of painkillers I suppose but they assure me I'll feel more comfortable now there's no risk of bone movement.'

'Fabulous.' Lisa emptied a bag of purchases on Helen's bed. 'Want to see what I bought today?'

Helen smiled as Lisa picked up an emerald-coloured blouse and held it against herself.

'I saw this in the window of a cute little shop and couldn't resist it. My size too!'

'Lovely.'

The display included drink coasters painted with Highland cows for her workmates, new tartan-backed gloves for herself, whisky glasses for her brothers, and two beautiful books full of photos of the Isle of Skye, one for herself and one for Tim's partner Heidi.

Ingrid arrived, her blonde ponytail swinging as she reached the bed and laid a gentle hand on Helen's. 'How's the patient?'

'I'm good thanks. The orthopaedic surgeon was lovely. So gentle and caring. And she spoke perfect English. I didn't realise she was Swedish until the nurse told me.'

They chatted for a few minutes before Helen's meal was delivered.

Helen lifted the lid and steam from the Cullen Skink rose to meet Lisa's nose as she leaned over.

'Oh, yum. That smells delicious!' Lisa's eyebrows rose.

Ingrid grinned. 'Come on, Lisa. We'd better get home. Callum will have dinner ready for me by now and I'm sure Lucy will be expecting you.'

'Yeah.' She gathered her purchases and kissed her mother. 'Ring me in the morning and I'll come and pick you up—if you're okay to be discharged that is.'

'Oh I will be,' Helen said confidently. 'I've already wasted three days of our holiday over this silly wrist, and I don't intend wasting a minute more.'

'Great. The day after tomorrow we're hiking to the Point of Sleat,' Ingrid said. 'And if you're up to it, Lisa and I'd love for you and Lucy to join us.'

Helen beamed. She would have to take things carefully as another fall could be devastating. But everyone said it was a relatively easy walk and not too long. At least it would fill their day and she would be able to think about something other than what was happening back in Australia. Her mind wandered for a second as Jack once again trespassed on her thoughts. She brought it back smartly and chided herself for comparing him to Michael—the skilled doctor who had assisted her on the hillside bore no comparison to her husband and had no place in her life. Or her heart.

Her thoughts seesawed.

I don't deserve another chance. But it would be nice to have a new friend.

Then, remembering his request for an update, she looked forward to making that call.

14

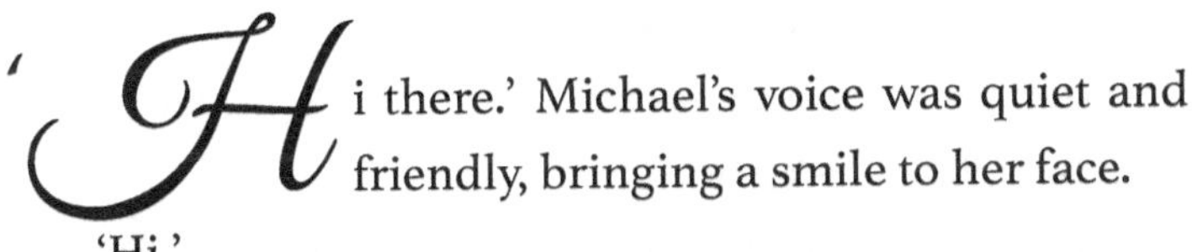

'Hi there.' Michael's voice was quiet and friendly, bringing a smile to her face.

'Hi.'

'How did it go?'

'Good thanks. No pain at all,' she said. 'I've got exercises to help with healing and other than that, I'm allowed to live life normally provided I don't attempt to lift anything heavier than a cup of coffee with that hand.' She ended with a chuckle, still astonished at the surprisingly straightforward instructions she had received following the surgery.

'That's great—and just how it should be.' There was a silent pause for a few seconds before he continued, 'I'd love to hear how the healing progresses—and how you're coping ... if you don't mind that is.'

'Of course. I'll send a text. Don't want to interrupt

with a phone call while you're with your son, but I appreciate your help and it would be nice to keep in contact.'

She hesitated again, stunned at the words that had just come out of her mouth. Uncertain of what to say next, she was relieved when he spoke first.

'I'll text you too—let you know what Scotland's like on the other side.'

'Thanks.'

'Well, I'd better let you get some sleep now. Enjoy a restful few days, and I look forward to seeing you when Julian and I get back to Skye.'

She thanked him again and said goodbye, then slowly lowered her phone.

Her body quivered with weird, unfamiliar emotions. Blinking rapidly, she attempted to examine them. They still hadn't exchanged any personal details except for his revelation that he had a son and was divorced. And, of course, he knew she had a daughter. So why then did she feel so ... different? Was this how normal friendships began? With the exception of Jack, she'd never had a friendship with a man—and what she and Jack had could have hardly been called a normal friendship.

Weariness engulfed her. She rearranged her pillow, lay back, her arm resting comfortably, and drifted into a dream-filled sleep.

THE VIBRATION of her phone dancing on her bedside table woke her. With eyes squinting in the semi-dark, she snatched it up, peered at the caller ID, and swiped the screen.

'Tim,' she whispered. 'It's the middle of the night. Is everything okay?'

'Sorry, Mum. I thought you'd still be awake.'

'I'm in hospital. They operated on my wrist yesterday and I'm staying the night. What time is it?' Fumbling with her good hand, she attempted to read the tiny digits on the top left-hand corner of her screen.

'It's eight o'clock in the morning here so I think it's eleven at night there. I need to ask you something and it's kind of urgent.'

Helen struggled to sit, turning her head away from the patient diagonally across the room. In the four-bed ward, two of the three other beds were empty. Hoping her roommate was a sound sleeper, she dropped her voice even lower. 'What is it?'

'I'm at Elizabeth Downs. Came over last night after I got a call from Clint. Apparently, he took someone to view the property a day or two ago and while they were inspecting the sheds, discovered a tarp-covered pile of iron sheeting and posts. It looks like a shed kit. Can't understand how Steve and I missed it, but I guess we were concentrating on the machinery when we did our audit and didn't think to look in that timber shed behind the trees.'

Helen was wide awake now, but she said nothing for a minute as she tried to recall the heap Tim had described.

'I don't know anything about a shed kit. Nor do I remember your father even mentioning a new shed—unless it was his intention to pull the old one down and replace it.'

'I thought that might be the case. Don't worry, Mum. I'll call the accountant and get him to check to see who it was purchased from. Then I'll ring whoever that is and see if they'll do a return. If that doesn't work out, I'll get one of the shed companies in town to value it and add it to the list to be sold—after we find a buyer of course.'

'The new owner of Elizabeth Downs—when we find him or her—might want to buy it.'

'True. Anyway, don't worry about it now. I'll sort it out. Just thought I'd better check with you in case it was something you wanted to keep.'

Helen blinked rapidly. 'If I knew where I'll be moving to, and if I needed a shed erected at wherever than ends up being, perhaps I might consider it. But honestly, love, I can't even think of those things at the moment. I just know we need a buyer. Then once I know how much money I'll end up with, I can take the next step forward.'

A groan sounded from the bed in the corner.

Helen grimaced, suddenly aware her whispers had become louder. 'Sorry, Tim. I'd better hang up now. Let me know how you get on.'

'Will do. Sorry I woke you.'

'It's okay,' she whispered. 'Bye now.'

'Bye,' he whispered back before the phone went silent.

She smiled softly. From his end, whispering was unnecessary but it brought back memories of when he was little and they would whisper to each other while they watched television so as not to disturb Jack. She'd turned it into a game. A secret language between Helen and her children—because when sport was on the television, any distraction or disturbance would anger Jack. Then they would all pay the price.

Snuggling back under the blanket, Helen's mind returned to Tim's discovery. A kitset shed? It was obviously bigger than a garden locker or Tim wouldn't be so concerned.

Her stomach flipped as she processed the issue. If Jack had bought a new shed and planned to erect it somewhere on the farm without discussing it with her, it could only mean one thing. He was up to something either illegal or immoral. Either way, it was not a good discovery. Dread unfurled inside her.

THE FOLLOWING morning under a blanket of grey, bleak clouds, Helen and Lisa arrived back at the annexe. Lucy greeted them with a hug then urged Helen to park herself on the couch while she made them a hot cup of tea and passed around a plate of freshly baked scones.

'Perfect timing,' Lucy said. 'Michael was right. I checked the weather radar and while the next couple of days look wet and wild for us, the eastern side of the mainland should be fine. Let's hope he and his son enjoy their walks before the rain reaches them.' She sighed. 'It will be a couple of days yet before we can think about our walk to the Point—sorry.'

'It's okay, Lucy. A bit more time spent puddling around here will be lovely.' Relief surged through Helen as she spoke.

While she enjoyed walking and had been looking forward to their hike, she'd felt surprisingly fragile since her fall and nervous about repeating it on slippery rocks. A couple of rainy days allowing her to rest and read sounded like heaven!

She'd slept well following Tim's call, but when she had woken periodically to adjust her position, it had been Michael who flashed through her thoughts.

Helen dismissed them once more, forcing her mind on Australia and focusing on the happy moments she and Jack had experienced on Elizabeth Downs. But even trying to seek the positives of life on the farm, they'd been so few and far between, she eventually gave up. Instead, she concentrated on the list of exercises the physiotherapist had run through with her that morning—determined that she would do everything she'd been told to do and be almost back to normal by the time she and Lisa got on the plane for home.

15

ith a cup of coffee in his hand, Michael scrolled through the emails that had arrived during the night, determined to devote his attention to Julian once he arrived.

He deleted the first few after casting his eye over them, then stopped. His chest tightening as he expanded the sender's address details. A law firm?

Narrowing his eyes, he checked the address again, expecting it to be another spammy one like those before it. But it wasn't.

Official claim documents have been posted to your Sydney address.

He scrolled to the bottom of the page, his pulse pounding. Attached was a copy of what he assumed was the document supposedly delivered to his home.

He opened it and read, his ex-wife's name jumping out at him.

Then he scanned the information again—certain he'd misunderstood it the first time—focusing on the part that shook every nerve in his body.

The legal jargon blurred in his mind. The names did not.

Mrs Anita Blakeney vs Doctor Michael Blakeney ... death of Amy Marion Blakeney.

He froze, counting to five before re-reading the details again.

Statement of claim ... Medical negligence ...

'Oh my God. Medical negligence? She's suing me for Amy's death,' he murmured.

An icy chill ran up his spine.

'I need a lawyer—now.'

16

Sydney, April 2023 – Michael

He was in the scrub room when Matt called code blue.

Michael rushed into emergency along with several other staff members, glancing from his colleague to the open cubicle at the far end.

'Over there. A young woman. Unconscious and triaged cat one,' Matt said as he bent over another patient lying prostrate on a gurney. 'Sonia's with her.'

Michael hurried into the cubicle, glancing first at the newest doctor in the department.

'Cardiac arrest,' she said. 'CPR in progress. Two lines are in. Adrenaline given. About to defib.'

'I'll take over airways.' Michael moved to the patient's head and halted. For a second he stared, wide-eyed at the pretty, fragile face.

'No!' His strangled cry filled the room. 'It's my daughter!'

His colleagues looked up in shock, all immediately cognisant of the implication for any health professional.

Sonia stared at him and spoke firmly. 'You can't be present. Please leave.' Turning back to the team, her voice deepened. 'Someone get Alan.'

Michael leaned against the wall outside the room, his heart thumping as a nurse rushed out seconds later before returning with Alan, another of his experienced colleagues.

The frenzied medical attention ramped up while Michael's head buzzed with panic.

'You can't die. You mustn't die,' he whimpered.

Minutes passed before the sound of running footsteps and breathless screams caught his attention, and he turned as Nita, his wife, approached.

'Where is she! Where's Amy? What's happened? Why aren't you doing something? You should be with her.'

A sudden anger crept over him—an emotion he rarely experienced. 'You know I can't diagnose or treat my own family. I've told you repeatedly. Emotions blur symptoms and it's unethical to do so. When you were worried, I told you to take her to our local doctor for a referral. Gave you names of specialists to seek for her treatment.' Heat flushed his face and neck. 'But, of course, it's much easier to blame me, isn't it?'

A nurse swooped in and guided Nita into a side room, shooting Michael a pitying look as she passed by him.

'She's a sixteen-year-old girl,' Nita shouted. You can't let her die! It's your fault,' Nita screeched as she pointed her finger at him.

Time stood still while Michael waited in the corridor. Eventually, a gentle arm on his made him look up.

'I'm sorry, mate,' Alan said. 'We did everything we could.'

'But I didn't! I didn't do enough. She's my daughter and now it's too late.'

HE BARELY FELT his colleague pull him to his feet, his arm under his, guiding him into the room where Nita sat beside a nurse, her face white.

'Michael?'

He looked into her disbelieving eyes.

'Is it true? Is it Amy?'

He nodded, unable to speak.

A long, tortured wail sounded from somewhere deep inside her as she slid off the chair onto the floor. In a daze, he knelt beside her, his arm wrapped around her shoulders. She turned to him and hid her face against his scrubs, the wails morphing to loud, hiccup-ping sobs.

He wanted to cry with her, to throw himself on the ground in a ball and beat his fists against the walls, the floor, or anyone who came near.

But he didn't. Little by little, he withdrew, silently, stoically building a wall around himself that no one, not even his wife, could penetrate.

He barely registered the social worker's visit—or their escorted stumble into a side room to say goodbye to their precious daughter.

The medical superintendent's hushed tones, voicing his sympathy and advising him another consultant had arrived to relieve him of his duties came from miles away. 'You are free to take your wife home and be with family.'

A brief nod of acknowledgement was all he could manage.

Minutes later, with his arm around Nita's waist, they staggered to the car, his anger spent.

He opened the passenger door and helped her into the seat, then, before moving around to the driver's side, he kissed the top of her head.

'I'm so, so sorry,' he said again.

She said nothing but raised her gaze to meet his.

He recoiled. His loving wife. The mother of his children. The woman he'd lived with for thirty years.

Unrecognisable.

There was no love. No sorrow. There was only one emotion that burned on her face—pure hatred.

17

———

*S*cotland, May 2025 – *Michael*

Michael and Julian hugged, Michael's joyful smile meeting his son's weary one.

'Jeez, Scotland's a long way from Australia, isn't it,' Julian grumbled.

Michael reached for the suitcase. 'Certainly is. Not the sort of flight you want to be hopping on and off too often.'

Julian rolled his shoulders and adjusted his rucksack. 'Do I get a rest before we set off on the first walk?'

Michael laughed. 'I thought you might feel that way. Let's head east and have a bite to eat. We'll check into the B & B and sort out the next couple of days' plan ... and then you can sleep.'

'Great. I feel like I've been locked in a cupboard for a week.'

Michael rolled his eyes and grinned again. 'I know, mate. It's rough but you'll feel better tomorrow, and once we've walked for a few hours, your bones will be back to normal.'

Julian shot him a doubtful grimace as they reached the car.

Michael placed the suitcase in the boot and lifted his gaze to the sky. Like paint streaks on an old footpath, grey clouds spread above them, a sliver of sunshine shafting through a gap. 'Good sign. Hopefully tomorrow will be a great day for hiking.'

Julian nodded silently and climbed into the car. 'Let's go. I can't promise I'll be stimulating company though.'

Michael put the car into gear and negotiated his way onto the motorway to Stirling. Delighted that he'd not only been able to speak to the author of the book that had kept him enthralled on Skye, but he'd also discovered that very same author and his wife owned and operated a B & B. So, he'd made an immediate booking and was looking forward to George joining him and Julian for their two days of hiking in the Cairngorms.

Despite Julian's exhaustion, the pretty scenery appeared to spark his interest as he made comments about the lush lowlands and stunning highlands. He chatted all the way to the village of Auchterarder, sharing details of his recently completed locum position, the possibility of moving to Queensland—'In my time off, I could explore the national parks. I've pretty much done all the climbs and hikes that I've wanted to in New South Wales'—and the woman who'd sat beside him on the long, tedious hours in the air. 'She was interesting—a university professor who travels all over the world teaching others how to write curriculum.'

Michael shot his son a surprised glance—astounded with Julian's observations. *Remember, he's not a kid any more.* 'Lovely,' he said.

By the time they entered the warm and welcoming pub, Julian appeared to have exhausted his barrage of chatter, switching his focus to a tasty hot meal and a mug of cider.

Dabbing his mouth with a serviette after scoffing a generous portion of venison casserole and chips, Julian frowned across the table. 'You're quiet, Dad. Something bothering you?'

Michael shook his head. 'Nothing much.'

'That sounds ominous. Can you tell me?'

'It's just something that happened at the hospital a couple of years ago. I got an email about it yesterday.'

Narrowing his eyes, Julian persisted. 'O ... kay. Why the delay if it's something that happened a while ago?'

Michael took a deep breath and placed his elbows on the table, resting his chin on interlaced fingers. 'I suppose some people take a while to process stuff—

and you never know who they've been talking to. Sometimes it only takes a disgruntled parent to trigger a barrage of questions about a patient's care. In this case, it feels more like a vendetta.'

'Cripes.'

Determined to push the hostilities away and concentrate on enjoying his time with Julian, Michael slid his chair back. 'Another drink?'

'No thanks. I'll probably drop off to sleep.'

'Righto. Let's get to the B & B. It's only a few minutes away.'

Relieved his son hadn't pushed for more information, Michael gathered his jacket and waited while Julian collected his before following him out the door.

AFTER A DELIGHTFUL EVENING with their hosts and a good night's sleep, the men set off early the next morning for Aviemore, grateful to be chauffeured by George, a giant of a man with the stride of an antelope.

Beginning at one of the main roundabouts in the thriving town, they marched northwards, the urban roads eventually meeting pretty countryside where they breathed easier having left the hustle and bustle behind. Pushing on across country and along old roads that were nothing more than tracks, they paused for regular breaks, leaning on their packs while they swallowed water and nibbled on the delicious food George's wife had provided. While George kept up an informative and entertaining tale of the effort he had put in to research, explore, and document the historic route, Michael's respect for the man soared, and the solicitor's letter faded to the back of his mind. He couldn't recall anyone who'd tackled a task as arduous as this one—or as interesting.

A sense of relief washed over him as they returned to the car late that afternoon, tired, damp, and exhilarated. Although they didn't reach Slochd Summit, as listed in the book, George had led them along paths that returned to the start of the walk to save having to camp out overnight. The fourteen-mile hike over a variety of terrain had been enough to whet Michael's appetite for more and, despite his initial goal to hike the steeper, challenging Munros of the Cuillin Mountains, he decided that one day, perhaps on another trip to Scotland, he would rejoin George and they would spend days enjoying the beauty of the Cairngorms on foot.

He glanced at Julian as his son threw his lithe, youthful body on the back seat.

'You alright, mate?'

'Sure am. That's what I call a good cure for jet lag.'

Laughing, they stowed their gear in the boot and began the drive back to the village.

Grateful for the continuing conversations about all

things hiking, history, and Scotland, thoughts of Helen suddenly popped into his mind.

I wonder how she is now.

Her soft, tanned face suddenly faded as a vision of Amy's beautiful, youthful smile replaced it. He pressed his weary body against the passenger seat as a sense of foreboding filled his insides.

18

———

$\mathcal{H}$elen and Lisa had been on Skye for almost two weeks when the four-day run of high winds stopped howling, the rain eased, and a watery sun appeared.

It was Wednesday and on the upcoming Friday night, a ceilidh was to be held at the nearby hotel in Isleornsay.

'No one should visit Scotland without experiencing a genuine ceilidh,' Lucy announced as she pointed to Helen's wrist. 'Even those with an injury.'

Helen grinned, shaking her head. 'I'm being very obedient and doing my exercises—so except for lifting heavy objects, I consider myself back to normal.'

They laughed and Helen stared through the window. 'If that's the case, perhaps tomorrow we could walk to the Point of Sleat?'

Lucy raised an eyebrow as she set the iron to the side and hung the shirt she'd been pressing on the door handle. 'Of course. It'll make a nice change and ...' she shot a wry grin at Helen, 'didn't Michael say he and his son were coming back today? Perhaps they'd like to join us?'

Feeling the heat rise on her cheeks, Helen turned back to the view through the window. Gulls were circling above the calm, blue water, the sun above providing streaks of gold on the green fields. She released a contented sigh. It was so beautiful here. Far from the dust, stress, and loneliness she'd endured for so long, she could barely remember how things had been before she married Jack. Happy in her solitude, she admired the confident, the outgoing, and those who made friends easily. But she wasn't one of them. By keeping to herself, she'd gotten through each day and had done her best to prevent conflict in her life.

Perhaps that's where I went wrong. Perhaps if I'd stood up for myself more, things would have been very different?

As though determined to crush her nostalgia before she let it drown her, her phone rang and she reached for it, her hand hovering above the name flashing on the screen—Michael Blakeney.

She snatched it up and swiped the icon. 'Hi there.'

'Hello.' There was a smile in his voice.

'How were things in Aviemore?'

'Lovely, thanks. The weather was a bit showery but nothing like you guys had here it seems.'

They exchanged weather details before Michael paused.

Helen looked up at Lucy, who was waving at her. 'Lucy wants to say something. I think her interrupting our calls is becoming a habit,' she laughed.

'Ask him to come for dinner—bring Julian and tell them about the ceilidh.'

Helen nodded. 'Did you hear that? Lucy wonders if you and Julian would like to come for dinner, and also there's a ceilidh at Isleornsay on Friday night which, apparently, no one should miss.'

'Sounds lovely. What night for dinner?'

'I'll check.' Helen lowered the phone to her lap and hissed at Lucy, 'What night for dinner? Tonight or tomorrow?'

'Make it tonight. Then we can discuss the walk tomorrow and see if they want to join us.'

Helen nodded and lifted her phone to her ear. 'Tonight?'

'Sounds great. We'll be there at ... say, six-thirty?'

'Perfect.'

After ending the call, Helen met Lucy's knowing smile.

'Lisa and Fergus will be in for lunch shortly. Let's get organised. We cooked lamb last time they came for dinner. How about venison or fish this time?' Lucy said.

Helen shrugged. 'Both sound fabulous so it's your choice.'

In the end, determined that Michael and Julian experience traditional food, they decided on a small serving of Cullen Skink each for entrée and venison and orange casserole with roast potatoes and wilted greens for mains.

'And I can make my healthy chocolate and chia seed mousse for dessert,' Helen said. 'It's time I did more to help. You've waited on me like an invalid for days now,' she finished firmly.

'Fair enough.' Lucy turned away as the back door opened and Fergus and Lisa walked in. There was a stalk of hay in Lisa's hair, and both smelled of sheep.

Fergus's bulk dwarfed Lucy as he gave her a hug.

An unexpected ache settled inside Helen. Their love was so evident ... so heartwarming. She straightened, swallowing the bitter reminders of her failed marriage that chose to appear when she least expected them, and plastered a smile on her face.

'Toasted sandwiches okay for lunch? Michael and his son are coming for dinner so I'm keen to have a lesson in creating some special Scottish delicacies.'

Lucy chuckled as she extracted herself from Fergus's bear hug. 'I'd hardly call Cullen Skink and a venison casserole delicacies, but I'll take the compliment. These are dishes Peggy taught me to cook when I returned here last year, and I'm delighted to be able to pass on what I've learned.'

'I'll just scrub up,' Lisa said, her face flushed with a healthy pink glow. 'Chasing those recalcitrant ewes and lambs was a bit muddy after the rain.' She glanced down at her mud-splattered jeans, still tucked into knee-length socks.

'Don't bother being too fussy, lass,' Fergus said. 'We've got one more lot to drench this afternoon and they won't be any cleaner than this morning's flock.'

'We'll ask Michael and Julian to join us at the ceilidh,' Lisa said. 'How old is he?'

'Who? Julian?' Helen replied.

'Yeah. I mean, is he in school holidays or what?'

Helen raised her eyebrows. 'I have no idea—but I reckon he'll be around your age.' She turned to Lucy. 'Didn't he say he was a vet?'

Lisa snapped to attention. 'Really? How come I didn't know that?'

'Probably because you were too busy thinking of other things,' Lucy said with a laugh. 'Like rushing back to the lambing shed.'

Lunch was prepared and eaten without hurry but by the time Helen had stacked the dishwasher and extracted the ingredients to begin preparation for dinner, butterflies were swirling in her stomach.

'We'll get the casserole in the oven first—let it cook

slowly all afternoon and it will melt in our mouths,' Lucy said.

Helen nodded, following Lucy's instructions with as much concentration as she could muster—which obviously wasn't enough when Lucy quirked an eyebrow and reminded her to scrub the vegetables before chopping them. Silently chastising herself, Helen finished the potatoes then focused on finding the ingredients for the mousse.

An hour later, with the evening meal prepared, Lucy announced they should go for a walk—just the two of them. 'To clear our heads so we can better enjoy our evening.'

Taking the track leading to the hills behind the croft, both women ambled in silence. At the top of the rise, they paused, panting.

Lucy pointed to a large rock beside the track. 'Let's sit down for a bit and enjoy the peace.'

Helen perched on a small flat section of the rock, stretching her long legs in front of her. She had always been the tallest and most solid of the trio of friends from boarding school days—Helen, Lucy and Roslyn. Even as a growing teenager, she had noted with envy the slim, lithe build Lucy appeared to have inherited from her father. Roslyn's petite frame and athleticism had contrasted with the stout figures of her parents, and they'd joked about her quick, darting actions being more like the tiny birds in the school trees than anyone else in her family.

Helen sighed. If it hadn't been for her strength, both physically and mentally, over the past forty years, she doubted she would be here now, overlooking the glistening, sun-streaked waters of the Sound of Sleat.

'I'm so sorry I didn't write to you more often.' Lucy's voice was soft, apologetic.

Helen shook her head sadly. 'It's okay. You were travelling overseas, and I was busy. Being unhappy wasn't the sort of thing we wrote about. Much easier to let everyone think life was sweet and having a baby arrive at three regular intervals was confirmation of that.'

'Did you feel pressure to marry him?'

'God!' Helen exclaimed so forcefully that Lucy's eyes widened. 'Pressure is an understatement. Both his parents and mine wouldn't hear of anything else. I was eighteen and should have known better—even though it was the 1980s not the 1950s! When I discovered I was pregnant, I considered a termination. But I couldn't do it. I believed my beautiful little boy was conceived in love! Huh. Lust more like. Anyway, I never could lie and even though Jack was a troublemaker and not exactly marriage material, I didn't want to hurt my parents any more than I had to. Dad was such an old-fashioned stickler for protocol and with his Greek upbringing, family meant everything. Mum ... well, I think she agreed with Dad—that marriage and babies brought endless happiness to every woman.'

'It can be hard growing up in a small country town, can't it?' Lucy grimaced.

'You're not wrong. And once you're entrenched like I was, I was too busy and too tired to consider doing anything about it. Living with Jack was like riding a roller-coaster for years on end and when he died, I felt I was finally being set free.' Helen turned her face to her friend's as she finished the sentence, waiting for the outraged expression.

But it didn't come.

Instead, Lucy reached out a hand and clasped hers. 'I understand.'

And as their eyes met, Helen knew she truly did.

19

The warm afternoon sun beat down on Lisa's back as the men closed their car doors and walked toward the croft, their eyes hidden behind sunglasses.

Her freshly washed hair hung over her shoulders and the barest hint of makeup enhanced a healthy glow on her face.

'Hi there! Come in.'

She stood back as Michael and Julian removed their shoes. Julian held out his hand and Lisa grasped it, hoping the men couldn't hear her heart thumping. Michael's son was not the spotty-faced teenager she had expected. Nor did he bear any resemblance to the vets she worked with—mostly mid-forties to nearing retirement. This man was tall, slim and, except for the lack of grey peppering his dark hair, even better looking than his father. They both had eyes the colour of the ocean on a sunny day, accentuated by dark eyebrows and lashes, only Michael's were now surrounded by smile lines while Julian's were almost crease-free.

They padded into the living room in their socks and while greetings were exchanged, Lisa practiced a few slow breaths, silently instructing her pulse to settle down.

From that moment, as the sun slowly slid toward earth and twilight hung over the isle, the evening just got better.

Lisa barely tasted the meal and was pleased that Lucy enlightened everyone that the tasty creations were Helen's, not hers. *Lord knows Mum needs all the reassurance possible after what our father put her through.* Praises were shared as the conversation danced from common subjects such as the weather, to the walks the men had done on the mainland, the improvement of Helen's wrist—'I'm sure it's the exercises'—she'd said, the upcoming ceilidh, and the next day's plan to hike to the Point of Sleat.

When the evening ended, an unexpected stab of excitement fizzed through Lisa. While she and Julian had engaged in general conversation, the following day's hike promised an opportunity to get to know each other better—and she looked forward to that.

THE MORNING DAWNED SOON after four-thirty as it had every other morning since their arrival, but for once Lisa didn't pull the covers over her head or curse the birds for singing. Instead, she crept out of bed quietly and headed for the shower. By five o'clock, she'd made both herself and Helen a mug of coffee, prepared sandwiches, and packed their rucksacks.

They had eaten breakfast and were sipping their second hot drink when Lucy tapped on their door.

'Are you nearly ready?'

'Sure are.' Helen rolled her eyes toward Lisa. 'Someone seems to be rather excited about today—can't think why.'

Lucy chuckled. 'Well, I'm thrilled you and Julian got on so well, Lisa. You have a lot in common—and there's no doubt he takes after his father in more ways than just manners.'

Lisa ducked her head. The bolt of attraction that had swept through her was an unfamiliar emotion. She'd had a few boyfriends but very early in her dating life had decided there was no point in spending unnecessary money and time with someone who showed more interest in her body than her brain—not that there was something wrong with a man who clearly admired her figure. But her father's behaviour and temperament had coloured her opinion of men so she preferred to take things a little slower, hoping that one day someone would appreciate her in other ways. She wasn't plain but was self-conscious of her wide hips and slightly slanted eyes, a legacy of her heritage. Not certain that "the one" would arrive any time soon, she'd put her career ahead of anything else and bonded more firmly with the animals she cared for than the humans in her life. But now ...?

She shook off the thought and sat down to lace her hiking boots while Lucy and her mother pondered over which jackets they should take if the glorious day unfolding outside should turn cold, wet, and windy.

At eight o'clock, as arranged, Lucy, Helen, Fergus, and Lisa, met Michael and Julian in the car park at the beginning of the track.

A local farmer was drafting sheep at nearby yards, and Fergus called a greeting. 'Lovely day for it.'

The farmer gave a wave and returned the greeting in the accent Lisa was learning to love. 'Aye. A grand one. Enjoy your walk.'

Lucy announced Callum and Ingrid were also joining them, explaining that Ingrid had messaged early to say she had the day off and wondered what everyone was doing. 'So I invited them to join us,' Lucy finished. 'And as you can see, here they are!'

As she finished speaking, the two of them arrived in a flurry of apologies for being a few minutes late.

Greetings were exchanged as they hoisted their rucksacks on and Callum and Ingrid struck out briskly, leading the group along the wide gravelled track and up the first hill. A few metres behind them, Julian fell in beside Lisa, Michael joined Helen, and Fergus clasped Lucy by the hand as they followed the team, swinging their arms as they walked.

Above, the last of the clouds disappeared and before they'd hiked the first mile, they had to stop to remove a layer of clothing.

After a number of stops to admire cotton-grass flowers and early flowering heather, sip some water, and take in the scenery, they trudged along the trail, eventually reaching a boundary fence where the track turned and a single-file clamber over rocks was required.

'Nearly there,' Callum called to them as he shot up the steep pinch like a gazelle.

Following them, Michael said quietly, 'Helen, I'm right behind you. Just go steady now.'

The exchange warmed Lisa more than the exercise did. She and Julian shared a knowing grin. It may have been only weeks since her had father died, but her mum deserved to be respected and cared for, and if Michael's encouragement helped Helen to regain both confidence and happiness, then she was all for it.

At the top of the ridge, they paused, staring across

the water to where the bulky Isle of Rum dwarfed the smaller Isle of Eigg.

'It's a shame we haven't got time to visit the small isles,' Lisa said wistfully. 'I've seen photos and they look so pretty.'

'Fergus invited Dad to join him on a boat trip to Rum. Apparently, a friend of Fergus's has a cottage there—rents it out to visitors I believe.'

'And he's going?'

Julian shrugged. 'I guess so. Not sure though.' He paused, a frown forming on his brow. 'It looks like there's a possibility he'll have to return to Australia sooner than planned.'

Lisa's gut clenched with disappointment. Her mother and Michael seemed so content, their relaxed stride echoing their easy banter. She couldn't remember Helen ever looking so tranquil—certainly not in the last decade or two anyway. With the exception of Shelley and her husband, Bill, her mother had few friends—only work associates from the charity shop and restaurant kitchen, and with those she had remained tight-lipped and distant. Under her father's reign, there had been a silent agreement that what occurred within the boundaries of Elizabeth Downs, remained there. Guests were not welcome, except for those visiting purely for agricultural reasons.

She shuddered, shed memories of the past, and followed Julian down the eastern side of the track to where, surrounded by rocks and wildflowers, sheep basked in the sun. Beyond the soft green grass, a pristine sandy beach glistened.

'Wow! How gorgeous,' Helen said, stopping beside Lucy and waiting for the others to catch up.

For several minutes, Fergus and Callum shared their experiences of the area as they'd grown up, told tales of local bountiful fishing expeditions and included the occasional mishap during wild weather.

Walking on, stopping to take photos as they went, Lisa and Julian were the first to reach the edge of the sand, having overtaken Callum and Ingrid when they diverted to inspect a break in the fence.

Julian shrugged off his pack and lowered it to the ground before helping Lisa remove hers. Then he took her hand and pulled her to the edge of the sand.

'Shall we?'

She smiled, unsurprised at his ability to read her mind. 'Let's.'

Together, they crossed the soft, dry sand rippled by the previous day's wind then with Julian counting down 'Three, two, one!' they jumped, laughing as they landed side by side on the smooth, pristine surface of untouched beach.

Lucy's laughter filled the air as she and Fergus approached. 'That's usually Fergus's and my trick. You beat us to it.'

Helen and Michael wandered toward them. 'Good

to see you're still kids at heart,' Michael said, smiling. He turned to Helen. 'When Julian and ... um, Julian was little, we lived close to the beach, and he loved me taking him down there early each morning so he could be the first person to press footprints in the sand.' He chuckled. 'Of course, he never was—someone always beat us to it. Usually a dog walker so there were not only human prints, but dog's as well.'

A hint of surprise crept over her mother's face. Had she also caught the slight hitch in Michael's words? Had he had been about to add another person's name?

'We're going to have a cuppa now,' Lucy announced. 'We won't join you to the lighthouse this time. You're fitter than I am, and I've been plenty of times.'

'I think I'd like to sit this one out too, if you don't mind?' Helen said.

Michael peered at her, frowning. 'Are you alright?'

'Yes, I'm fine. But I know I've got to walk back yet and it's rather nice sitting here soaking up the beauty.'

Michael nodded and waved Lisa and Julian away. 'I reckon we'll just perch awhile here. You two enjoy yourselves and if you're not back within an hour, I'll come looking for you.'

Julian swung his rucksack onto his back again, grinning at Lisa, as Callum called to them, 'You two go on. We're going to fix this broken fence. It's not our land but a good turn for neighbours never goes astray.'

'Okay,' Julian called. 'We'll be back.' Then he and Lisa headed along the sand to the far end of the beach, picking over the tiny shells and laughing as they evaded the gentle waves stroking the beach.

Reaching the headland, they clambered over rocks and the rest of the group disappeared from sight.

20

The distance to the modern, steel-framed lighthouse wasn't far but the walk was strewn with boulders and rocks of every size and shape, taking more time than Lisa had expected. Following their arrival, they explored the unusual structure then sat opposite each other, Julian on a flat chunk of granite and Lisa on a dry, scrubby heather bush.

She pulled a sandwich from her pack and took a mouthful of water. 'I'm starving!'

He laughed and removed a well-used paper bag from his rucksack. 'Me too.'

They munched quietly, Lisa's mind fleeing back to Michael's reference to taking Julian on the beach years earlier.

'Are you an only child?' she asked.

'No. Well, sort of. I had a sister but she died.'

'Oh!' Lisa cringed. 'Sorry. I shouldn't have asked.'

'That's okay. It's hard to believe we only met yesterday. I feel like I've known you for ages—and I'm happy to share stuff with you if you'll tell me a bit about yourself?'

'Hmm. Not much to tell really.'

'So ... you tell me and then I'll share more about my life.'

'Okay. I grew up on Elizabeth Downs in Queensland with my two brothers and Mum and Dad. Mum's great. Easy to live with, hardworking, and loves us kids to bits. Dad ... well, I don't remember too many good times. I guess they were there, but he was a hard man to live with. Loud, unpredictable, and when he lost his temper, which was often, he was terrifying.'

Julian's jaw dropped. 'Tough.'

She shrugged. 'Yeah, well. I guess that's why the boys and I couldn't wait to leave and weren't exactly heartbroken when he died—and why none of us want to go back there to live. Now, your turn.'

He shifted to a grassy patch and lay back, propped on his elbows.

'I've had a pretty cushy upbringing. Dad wasn't home much—being a doctor meant he worked long hours and was often on call. Mum owned a boutique ...

She's a bit of a fashion diva. Anyway, I had a wonderful grandmother who lived with us so didn't miss anything. Then, when I was twelve, my sister Amy arrived. She was born with a heart murmur—and was utterly gorgeous. Bright, pretty, and we all spoiled her rotten. I'd already gone to university when she started getting sick. Long story short, she became anorexic and despite getting all the help she could, she died ... two years ago.'

'Oh no!' Lisa's hand flew to her mouth.

'We were devastated. Gran had passed away only months earlier and Mum was so angry at Dad over Amy's health issues, and for not treating her. She never seemed to understand that it would've been unethical if Dad had—he would have lost his job and his right to practice. She demanded Dad move out, changed the locks, had a separation agreement done, and now they're divorced. Luckily, he and I've always been close so even though I was upset when it happened and didn't behave as kindly as I should have, we quickly regained our bond. The weird thing is, Dad's never been bitter. He blames himself for not helping Amy more and believes Mum's accusations are justified.'

'Does he still love your mother?'

He shook his head. 'I don't think so. To be honest, I think their relationship had been a bit strained for a while. Amy was a surprise baby. After I was born, they were told they couldn't have any more so I guess I'd been the typical spoilt brat before Amy arrived. Mum had post-natal depression after Amy's birth and put all her energy into her business, so it was largely Gran, with a bit of help from Dad and me, who cared for Amy for those first few years. I adored her. She was the sweetest little kid ever—until she reached fourteen, then things turned for the worse.' He slumped onto his back and, shading his eyes with a hand, gazed at the sky. 'I've been lucky in so many ways. Both my parents have always been loving and caring toward me. I don't see Mum often, but we get along well.'

She shuffled toward him and squeezed his hand. 'Thank you for telling me. It must have been a horrible time for you all—and I'm pleased you and your father are close.'

He lay an arm across her shoulders and pulled her to him. 'Thanks for listening.'

His warm body pressed against hers. They stayed in the position and time stood still for Lisa, not wanting to move. A sudden breeze lifted her ponytail and whipped it into Julian's face, breaking the precious interlude.

'What made you decide to be a vet?' Lisa asked.

'I wanted to be a doctor. Dad talked me out of it and because I loved animals and medical stuff, becoming a vet was the next best career. I've never liked living in the city so I'm enjoying doing rural locums.' He shook his head. 'I don't think I'll ever live in a city again if I can help it.'

Their smiles met and Lisa reluctantly pushed herself to her feet. 'I'm hearing you. Even though I enjoy working where I do—the big, busy vet practice— I miss being with large animals. When I got the job, I just wanted to get as far away from the farm as I could, and like heaps of other eighteen-year-olds, I suppose I thought the Sunshine Coast was a far more exciting place to live and work than boring old Clermont. But ... we mostly deal with cats and dogs and, like I said, I miss the horses and cattle. Give me a country practice any day,' she finished wistfully.

He reached out, and she pulled him to standing, her smile widening as Fergus's whistle sounded over the gentle lapping of the waves against the rocks.

'I think that's the signal. Time to return to the beach.'

He gave her a quick hug, sending a shiver of excitement through her. While still reeling from her father's abrupt death, she struggled to believe he'd been one in a million and that most men were normal, pleasant citizens. She adored her brothers—and neither had echoed the nasty temperament of their father. Perhaps she'd been too judgemental? Fergus, Michael, and now Julian had shown her how caring and gentle the opposite gender could be.

As she stared into the blue-grey eyes of her new friend and confidant, a deep warmth filled her heart.

I think I may have been too hasty.

THEY REJOINED the rest of the group, and the warm feeling inside Lisa deepened. She couldn't remember ever having seen her mother so relaxed and happy. Despite her fall, injury, and husband's death due to what may or may not have been an accident, encompassed by friends, the recent traumatic years appeared to have fallen away from her like the bark from a tree. Behind it, her mother, carer, and confidante was emerging—a brighter, smiling soul ready to tackle whatever came her way.

'How was the lighthouse?' Helen asked as they approached.

Lisa shot Julian a tender grin. 'Great. Not quite what we picture a lighthouse to be but it's definitely doing the same job, so I guess looks don't really matter.'

'Great views from up there too,' Julian added. 'Not sheltered like this lovely bay, but nice to visit.'

Everyone gathered picnic leftovers and repacked the rucksacks, chatting between themselves as they struck off on the return walk to the car park.

'I'm looking forward to tomorrow's ceilidh,' Julian

said as he unloaded their rucksacks back at Fergus and Lucy's croft.

'Me too,' Lisa said. 'It'll be fun. I hope you have enough energy after your day in the Cuillins to dance the night away?'

'I will.' He squeezed her hand as he passed her the backpack. 'I'll make sure of it. Maybe see you later?'

The glow that had warmed her all morning continued as they exchanged farewells and she ambled toward the annexe behind her mother.

'A cup of tea for me now, then I intend to have a quiet rest and read my book,' Helen announced.

'I'm hearing you, my friend.' Lucy smiled at them both. 'I'll get the curry on for dinner tonight and while it simmers, the book I'm dying to finish will be my next priority.'

'What are you reading?' Lisa asked.

'One that's been on my to-be-read pile for a while. It's called *The Quarantine Station*. It's written by an Australian author—Michelle Montebello—and it's so good! I don't want it to finish but I do want to know what happens.'

They all laughed as if totally understanding her feelings.

'And what about you, Lisa?' Lucy asked.

'I'm going to download my photos onto the laptop and catch up on some messages and emails. It's too nice a day to sit inside so once I've done that, I might even go for a drive.

She didn't miss the knowing look her mother and Lucy exchanged but she didn't care. Julian was the nicest guy she'd met in a long time—and from the attention he'd showed her both the previous night and today, she was certain he felt the same way about her.

21

———————

The day of the ceilidh dawned bright and sunny, the clear warm air once again lifting everyone's spirits.

While Lisa and Fergus headed to the lambing shed after breakfast, Helen joined Lucy in the garden where they inspected the bare patch of rich soil and extracted the weeds that had appeared since Fergus had dug it over three days earlier. Then, after much discussion, debate, and collusion, they crawled around the circular garden, planting the myriad of seedlings in neatly arranged order so that within weeks, the bed would be a thick swatch of summer-flowering plants.

'Having the delphiniums in the middle will provide a great backdrop for the smaller plants.' Helen stood with her hands on her hips as she surveyed their work.

'And I do like a mix of colours. I would love to grow flowers,' she finished wistfully.

Lucy shot her a sharp frown. 'I'm sure you will. You're a free woman, don't forget. You can do anything you want to do.' They both smiled at each other before Lucy continued, 'I went through a stage back home in Queensland where I would stick to a colour scheme each spring. You know, pink and white in one bed, blue and yellow in another.' She chuckled. 'Now I don't really care what colours they are. Summers here are so short compared to Australia, so I enjoy a mish-mash of whatever I can get to grow.'

She removed her gloves and inclined her head toward the house. 'Tea?'

'Perfect,' Helen said with a thoughtful sigh.

'I wonder how Michael and Julian are getting on in the Cuillins. So good that Callum could spare the time to join them. Nothing like having a local to share tips and history as you go.'

Following her friend inside, an unexpected surge of elation surprised Helen. On the walk the previous day, she had enjoyed Michael's company. Their discussions had been light, exchanging nothing more personal than their children's occupations, holidays—which was easy for Helen because she hadn't had a holiday for decades—animals, and their shared love of trees. However, throughout the walk, Helen had sensed there was something more Michael wanted to say.

Something serious. Perhaps it was something too personal to share at this stage of their friendship, she'd wondered. *Whatever the reason, he obviously isn't able to —at least not yet.*

She'd felt a flicker of disappointment but admitted she hadn't been any more open than he was. With the police still investigating Jack's death, too many questions hung in the air. Was it suicide? An accident? Murder? And what was she supposed to do once she returned to Australia? She couldn't face going back to Central Queensland, yet nothing—and no one—was drawing her anywhere else.

'Tea or coffee?' Lucy asked, breaking Helen's train of thought.

'Oh ... coffee please.'

'I thought perhaps next week, seeing it's your last here, we might spend a couple of days on the mainland. I'd love to take you to the Inverewe Gardens— they're one of the best you'll ever see and if the weather stays like this, it will give us both inspiration for our own gardens. What do you think?' Lucy smiled brightly, unaware of Helen's internal dilemma.

'It sounds lovely, Lucy. I'm not sure that Lisa will want to come.'

'That's fine. If she doesn't, we'll enjoy a wonderful little break away on our own. I admit I haven't been off Skye for months and it will be good to have some "girl time" together.' She mimed the quotation marks with fingers in the air and they both laughed.

'Girls?' Helen snorted. 'It's been a long time since I felt like a girl. These days it's more like an old mare trying to keep up with the younger generation—and the workload.'

'Well then. It's time we changed that.' Lucy said matter-of-factly, ending the topic. She poured the coffee and opened a packet of chocolate biscuits. 'Let's take it outside.'

Helen nodded and followed her around to the southern side of the house where a small, sheltered alcove held a ceramic-topped table and two comfortable chairs.

'About tonight,' Helen began. 'Do we need to prepare food? Help with set up?'

'I'll bake something for supper this afternoon. Maybe I'll break with tradition and, instead of something Scottish, make one of Adam's favourites—sausage rolls with sesame seeds on top and my home-made tomato dipping sauce.'

'Sounds delicious.'

Adam was Lucy's only child, now a man in his thirties with a wife and a baby on the way. Living on the farm where Lucy had grown up, Adam ran a thriving cattle and grain business with his cousin who lived on the adjacent property, providing Lucy—as part owner of "Binnalong"—with a relatively secure income.

'How is Adam? And his wife ... Meg, is it?'

'Yes. They're both wonderful. Meg's only got a few weeks to go before the baby arrives.'

'Will you come over to be with them?'

'Definitely!' They both laughed. 'The best thing we ever did after Mum died was to build the cabin. It was perfect for Dad—and for me when Adam and Meg married. It gives me my own little home where I can stay as often as I like—and for as long as I want to. Of course, I don't want to leave Fergus for too long. We waited thirty-four years to be together again, so every day is precious. But so is my first grandchild and Fergus totally supports me on that one. He'd like to come too, but it will depend on what needs to be done here.'

Each sat for a minute in silence before Lucy asked the question Helen had been waiting for and dreading ever since she'd arrived on Skye.

'What's next for you?'

She slumped into her chair, shaking her head slowly. 'I just don't know—and I guess I won't until the police have finished their investigations and the farm's sold. If it fetches a good price, hopefully there'll be something left over for me to put into a new place, even if it's tiny. But if it doesn't ...' She trailed off with a helpless shrug. 'I might be living with Lisa.'

'Surely not,' Lucy said in an alarmed tone. 'I mean,

we love our children dearly but is that really what you would both want?'

'Lucy! Life doesn't always work out the way we want it to.' Helen spoke more sharply than she'd meant to.

Reaching forward, Lucy placed her mug on the table and lay her hand on Helen's. 'I'm so sorry. I didn't mean to upset you. It's none of my business. But ... for everyone's sake, I hope the sale goes better than anyone dreamed of.' She picked up her empty mug again and rose. 'Now, I'd better get on with those sausage rolls.'

Helen didn't move, her insides curling with guilt at the tone she'd used with Lucy. She didn't deserve it. They were best friends. But Helen couldn't stop thinking about her future. If the farm made no profit or, worse still, was sold at a loss, her choices would be to live with one of her children—or in her car. And she was determined she would not let that happen.

HELEN WASN'T sure what to expect at a ceilidh, but within minutes it became clear they were very similar to the dances held in country halls all around Australia. A wide variety of music, dancing, good food, and dozens of smiling faces.

Michael and Julian had arrived at Fergus and

Lucy's half an hour early—'So we could tell you how good today's climb was,' Julian had said excitedly.

Both men were dressed in clean jeans, button-up shirts, and R.M.Williams boots, their hair still wet and smelling deliciously of shampoo and a hint of something even nicer. Their faces wore a pink sheen, as though the day's rays had warmed them a little more than they'd expected in this Scottish climate.

While Fergus handed around cold drinks, Michael and Julian took turns to relay the news of their positive day—one where nothing went wrong, the track had been better than expected, and they'd met another group of Australian hikers with whom they'd shared an abseiling experience—an unexpected but enjoyable twist to their plans.

'I hope you saved enough energy for an evening of dancing,' Fergus asked.

'Oh yes.' Julian looked directly at Lisa, who blushed. 'I could dance all night.'

Michael rolled his eyes as they met Helen's. 'Not sure about that. Don't think I'll be attempting to keep up ... but I'll do my best.' He smiled then, a wide, engaging grin that deepened the creases around his eyes and sent Helen's heart into flight mode.

22

———

For hours, the band played a bracket of Scottish reels and traditional dances interspersed with popular songs, keeping the crowd on their feet and smiles on everyone's face.

At ten o'clock, the music stopped and supper was served.

Michael placed his hand on Helen's back, steering her through the crowd to the chairs lining the walls.

She plonked herself down, her soul soaring with elation and a little relief. Michael was a good dancer, light on his feet, and seemingly oblivious to her tremulous efforts as they swung around in fours, eights, and then slowed for the occasional one-on-one breath-catching dances. Throughout every bracket, he had asked if she wanted to continue dancing, led her regularly to the bar for another cool drink, gently holding her hand and confirming her wrist was pain-free.

Feeling as though she was floating on a cloud, Helen searched for Lisa and Julian, who, on several occasions, had swirled past her laughing and singing along to the music. Jack had not been a dancer and whenever a community function had been organised and she had pressed him to attend, he'd spent most of the evening at the bar while she danced with their children and washed dishes for hours afterwards. They had not been the happy outings she'd dreamed of—at least not for her anyway.

Lucy slumped into the chair beside her, her face alight with joy, strands of her blonde-grey hair curling around her flushed face. 'Great fun, isn't it?'

Helen smiled at her and nodded. 'Wonderful.'

'Ready for something to eat?'

'I am but I told Michael I'd wait until he's back from the bathroom.'

'He's certainly been looking after you tonight, hasn't he?' Lucy said with a knowing smile. 'Nice guy.'

Filled with nervous doubt, Helen said nothing. Everything seemed too good to be true and she didn't want to break whatever the spell was that had brought him into her life. *I've got nothing to offer.* But what if their meeting was the beginning of the change she yearned for? Perhaps he was the good omen she needed?

Supper was eaten and dancing began again. The room was hot and her feet were aching so when Michael suggested they take a breath of fresh air, she willingly followed him outside.

Small groups of people were sitting at the tables and chairs scattered around the outdoor area while others strolled along the foreshore or sat on upturned dinghies and talked.

Side by side, Helen and Michael wandered to the end of the pier and sat on the wide concrete kerb, their feet dangling over the edge with the sea gently lapping the rocks below them.

'It's so beautiful, isn't it?' Michael breathed.

'Sure is. It will be hard to leave.'

'What will be waiting for you in Australia? Back to the farm?'

She shrugged. 'Probably. But hopefully not for long. It's for sale.'

Shooting her a puzzled frown, he reached out and squeezed her hand gently. 'I know your husband died recently but from what I've gathered from Julian and Lisa's snippets of conversation, it wasn't as devastating for you as I first thought.'

'You're right. I'm embarrassed to admit that losing him hasn't been all bad. Things had been rocky for years—decades even—and I was too weak or too stupid to do what I should have done. Left.'

'Don't blame yourself. We all do things we think are right at the time—and later, realise they weren't.'

She stared at him for a moment, empathy filling her soul. 'You sound as though you've been there?'

'Yep. My wife—ex-wife—had been concerned about Amy losing weight, but I thought it was a good thing. She'd been a chubby kid and had discussed healthy weight loss with me. So I thought that was all it was—a normal teenager wanting to fit in with her peers and look good. I suggested Nita take her to a doctor and get a referral to a specialist if necessary. Because of the long hours I worked, most of the time she was asleep when I got home—which is no excuse when it comes to your own kids but that's the way it was. We talked whenever we could, and Amy didn't exhibit anything that rang alarm bells with me. When she collapsed at school and was rushed to hospital—into my emergency department—it came as a shock.'

'Oh no! What happened?'

'The team couldn't save her. Her heart stopped while she was on the gurney and despite everything, she died.'

Helen reached out and wrapped her arms around his shoulders, her heart aching with such pain she thought it might break, just as his had obviously done. It was one thing to lose a husband who had caused fear and agony for years, but a million times worse losing a beloved child—especially when they'd died of a manageable condition.

They leaned on each other, Helen resting her head against Michael's shoulder while his tilted against hers. Michael drew in a deep breath and straightened. 'I'm sorry to have put that on you.'

'Don't be silly. I'm flattered that you were prepared to share such a tragedy. I can only imagine how you feel—and I understand your grief.'

'Thanks. I've always been a believer in time healing everything, but sometimes I'm not sure that's correct.'

'Was it your daughter's death that brought you here to Scotland? To get away from those demons?'

'Probably. I love my work but it's a heavy load to bear at times. I guess I was on the verge of a breakdown—and after Amy's death and Nita and I divorcing, that's the last thing I would want Julian to witness.'

They sat in silence, the sound of music and laughter wafting in the air seeming miles away.

Eventually Michael asked, 'Tell me more about you. Is your biggest concern now the farm?'

She groaned. 'Yes. The debts my husband owed—unfortunately without my knowledge—were considerable. I'm not sure how much I'll receive after the farm sells and they're paid out, but I'm hoping it will be enough to secure a home for myself somewhere, even if it's small and a long way from the coast.'

'Crikey. That's tough.' He stared at her helplessly, as

though digesting the information had created a blockage in his throat.

'Yep. I've lived on that farm since I was eighteen. Planted hundreds of trees, worked hard—in the old tractor in forty-degree heat with no air-conditioning, on horseback mustering cattle through the rough areas of our land, coping with drought year after year. But I love the farm. The open air, the wildlife and caring for animals, and protecting the country for future generations. It will be hard to leave. It's a weird feeling, but I've realised I'm ready to put Elizabeth Downs behind me.'

They exchanged a smile and she continued, 'I'm very lucky my kids arranged this trip for me. Supposedly to get away from the stress, catch up with my old friend, and have a chance to think things through.' She gave a tiny chuckle and held up her arm. 'The last thing I expected was to break my wrist—but the good part was meeting you—and Julian. Thank you.'

'You're welcome.' His smile widened before he grew serious again. 'Something's come up at home so I've had to change my flight and will be leaving on Tuesday. Julian will stay until the end of the week—then he, too, will head back to Australia.'

'Oh! Is it something serious?'

'Not sure—but I think it could be.'

'I'm sorry. Can we keep in touch?' she asked hesitantly, half-expecting him to sever their ties. With his busy life in Sydney and generous salary, she couldn't imagine why he or anyone would want to befriend her. Assuming he was like every other doctor she'd met who sent their children to private schools and took annual skiing or yachting holidays, she understood how her potential homelessness would put him right off.

'Of course. I'd like that. Seems we both need a friend.'

Her seesawing stomach settled for a moment, the butterflies pausing with delighted shock. Uncertain of whether it was the night air, the tiring hours of dancing, or something else, suddenly the heaviness sitting inside her floated away as he pulled her toward him in a long, tight hug.

She closed her eyes, breathing in his scent as she pressed her face against his neck.

It's early days, but I don't care what else happens—so long as we are friends and I get to feel like this again.

23

—————

Tuesday approached too quickly for Helen. While she and Michael had exchanged texts, the only opportunity for them to meet again had been on Sunday when they descended on Kinloch Lodge for lunch. It had been Fergus's suggestion, and both Lucy and Helen had jumped at the opportunity, their delight increasing when the others accepted the invitation to join them. So, on the dot of twelve, Fergus and Lucy, Callum and Ingrid, Michael, Julian, Lisa and Helen gathered around the table in the gracious dining room overlooking the water, ignoring the misty showers that darkened the skies outside.

There was no opportunity for one-on-one conversations, but the food and wine was consumed with gusto and the air filled with varied and happy chatter —until Fergus announced he'd arranged with his friend, Ken, to take the men out fishing on Monday. She clenched her hands together, shocked at the cloak of disappointment that engulfed her.

Helen chided herself for being so selfish—she didn't even like fishing. But secretly she'd hoped she and Michael would have more time to talk. Fixing a permanent smile on her face, she expressed her delight for them and gave herself a silent reprimand. *I came here to see Lucy and get my thoughts together. Meeting Michael has simply been a pleasant extra.* Reminding herself of these facts, she straightened and determinedly enjoyed every minute the group had together.

HEAVY CLOUDS HUNG over the sea as the four men motored away from the shore on Monday morning.

Although excited about having a day out fishing—something Michael had not done in years—his emotions swung from the high that dining with his new friends at Kinloch the previous after-noon had ended on, particularly when he and Helen had shared a goodbye hug, to a sense of foreboding as the call from Australia clouded his mind.

It wasn't only the distance between the two coun-tries that filled him with a sense of disconnection. As recollections of that dreadful day in emergency returned, he had gone over the scene a million times.

So, what happened?

Nita had been there. She knew that everything in his and his colleagues' power had been done to save their daughter. They'd stood together through the coroner's report, the funeral, and the tsunami of grief that followed. Why now? Two years after everything. Why did she want to put them both through it again? It didn't make sense.

Overwhelmed with misery and concern, he jumped as Fergus's deep voice resonated in his ear.

'I've baited your hook for you. Here you go.'

Michael grimaced an apology. 'Sorry. Mind was elsewhere.'

'Aye. Thought it might be. That's why we're here—to forget about what's going on in the world and concentrate on finding some good-sized fish for dinner while enjoying each other's company.'

Michael grinned then. Fergus was right. It was his final day on the isle and although the skies were grey, there was no wind, no rain, and he was surrounded by his new friends. It was time to put away all thoughts of what may be waiting for him when he returned to Sydney. He wanted to enjoy every last minute in Scotland.

Two hours of fishing passed surprisingly quickly. With the clouds lifting and seven large fish lying in the cold box, Ken restarted the motor and they puttered across the water to land on a pristine beach on the Isle of Rum.

Outside Ken's cabin, they lit a fire and cooked two of the fish. Then, with a cold drink each and the salads Lucy had prepared for them, they sat around a large wooden table and devoured their meal, talking, laughing, and sharing stories. For the first time, Michael and Julian heard Fergus's brief but emotional tale of how he'd lost Lucy. Then, miraculously, thirty-four years later, they had found each other again—thanks to Ingrid.

The sensitivity of the big man, and the obvious love and care he had for Lucy, shone in his every word. Michael's understanding of the bond Fergus and Lucy had with Ingrid also became clear. His insides twisted with compassion and admiration. To have loved someone so intensely and for so long, never wavering or accepting anyone else in his life, showed a spirit Michael envied.

He dipped his head, studying the ground without seeing any of it as thoughts filled his head. Fergus and Lucy's story also proved that second chances were possible.

I will remember that.

ollowing Lisa's decision to stay at Lucy's and join Julian to explore more during his final days on Skye, it was only Lucy and Helen who drove away on Tuesday morning.

Michael's parting text had lingered in Helen's thoughts throughout the night, leaving her restless and flat by morning. She hadn't felt so dispirited since leaving home. Perhaps a brief escape—somewhere new in Scotland—would help ease the weight of his farewell.

After crossing the Skye bridge, they headed to Eilean Donan Castle where they wandered around the grounds taking photos and absorbing the history. Then, driving north to the Wester Ross area, they followed the road through picturesque countryside to Loch Carron. Cold winds and lashing showers kept them hopping in and out of the car to take snaps and admire the sights until they reached the small village of Sheildaig where they enjoyed a flask of tea while overlooking the loch. Listless and confused by her feelings, Helen stared through the window as they continued through intermittent showers to Gairloch, where they nestled into the cosy B and B cottage.

It wasn't until later that evening after they'd enjoyed a hearty meal at the local hotel and were comfortably stretched out on their beds that Lucy raised the subject of Helen's future again. 'Have you thought any more about where you want to live when you return home?'

'I haven't stopped thinking about it,' Helen said, huffing out a breath. 'I know where I don't want to live —but that doesn't help much.'

About to share her desire for a small cottage with enough garden space to grow masses of flowers, Helen jumped, snapping her mouth shut when her phone rang. She picked it up and frowned at the caller ID. 'Private number.'

'Don't answer it,' Lucy said.

But it was too late. Helen had already swiped the green icon. She tapped the speaker and held the phone away from her to allow Lucy to also listen to the conversation. 'Hello?'

'Is that Mrs Helen Gooding?' The voice was brisk and deep.

'Yes,' she answered tentatively. 'Who is this?'

'Detective Senior Sergeant Russell Seal, Queensland Police. I'd like to talk to you about an incident that took place on the property you and your late husband own. Elizabeth Downs.'

Helen's eyes widened as she glanced across at Lucy. 'Yes.'

'I'm in charge of the investigation into your husband's death.'

'I've completed a statement,' she retorted, regretting her brisk tone as soon as the words were out.

The detective's voice softened a little. 'It has been passed on to my department and I'd like to talk to you more about what happened that day. Would it be possible for me to visit you at your farm?'

'I'm in Scotland.' Stunned, she couldn't contain the wariness in her voice.

'Oh! I apologise. I didn't realise you were out of the country.' He paused for a beat. 'When will you be returning?'

'This weekend. I expect to be back on Elizabeth Downs by next Monday.'

'I see.'

There was another lengthy pause while Helen's pulse raced.

Helen plucked nervously at the bed sheet. 'Is there a problem?'

'We'd like to confirm your movements that day. I

understand you were not at home at the time of the incident but there is no validation of where you were?'

Lucy gasped, her eyes widening as Helen stared at her in alarm.

She swallowed and straightened her shoulders. 'I was at work—until I was asked to drive a sick colleague home. I dropped her at her house as she wasn't well enough to drive.'

'Then where did you go?'

'Home to Elizabeth Downs. I'm sorry, Detective. It's late at night here. Can we talk when I get back to Australia?'

He grunted apologetically. 'Of course. Sorry to have bothered you. I'll be here next Monday. Perhaps we could continue this conversation then?'

'Yes. Thank you.' Helen disconnected the call and met Lucy's wide-eyed gaze.

'Do they suspect you're responsible for Jack's death?' Lucy's voice rose with incredulity.

Helen shrugged.

'That's preposterous. You're such a tolerant person.' Lucy snorted a tiny laugh. 'How you stayed living in those awful circumstances for so long is hard to comprehend.'

Helen dropped her gaze to her hands, inspecting the rough skin and raised veins that, regardless of wearing gloves for every possible task, were becoming more noticeable with age. Her mouth dropped open as recollections of the day returned. 'I've just remembered—I didn't go straight home after dropping Sally off,' she whispered.

'Where did you go?'

'There's a side road near Sally's farm that goes through the bush and stops at a waterhole. I used to take the kids there to swim when they were small. It's quite deep and had one of those rope swings on an overhanging tree then—it's gone now. The children loved pretending to be Tarzan and as we only had a couple of farm dams which were strictly for the stock and I didn't have the money to take them to the town pool, it was the nearest place I could find to teach them to swim and have fun during the really hot days.'

'So why did you go there after dropping Sally off?'

'To sit quietly and enjoy the peace. No one seemed to visit the waterhole after the kids grew up and sometimes, when life wasn't too busy, I would take myself there to ... well, just think about things. The water attracted so many birds. I loved watching them—they were a beautiful distraction.'

Her vision blurred as she reminisced. 'Kookaburras came down to fish and rainbow bee-eaters nested in the banks. I stayed deathly quiet, so they seemed content to have me there.'

'And how long were you there before you went home?'

Helen met Lucy's gaze, her brow furrowed. 'I really

don't know. Half an hour? Maybe an hour? Jack and Warren were busy harvesting and I'd told Jack I'd be at work. We never knew what time I'd finish you see. Sometimes it was when the wait staff arrived around five and sometimes it was an hour or two later. I always left dinner prepared at home, so Jack didn't bother asking.' She shrugged. 'I don't think he really cared. When I got home, he'd usually be watching sport on TV and drinking beer or be working in the shed. But that day, I'd finished the evening vegetable prep and done the other little jobs I was responsible for. The kitchen was spotless, so when Sally—she's the lady who does reception and accounts a couple of days each week—told me she was feeling ill, our boss suggested I finish early and drop her at her place on my way home.' Her voice faded. 'I'd forgotten about my visit to the waterhole. There was so much chaos at home when I arrived that the whole day became a stressful jumble of emotions.'

Helen shuffled down in the bed and stared at the ceiling. She could feel Lucy's eyes on her and clenched her teeth to stop her lips from quivering. Lucy was easygoing and saw the best in everyone. But the more Helen thought about what she'd just told her, the less she wanted to look at her. An icy chill crept up her spine, fear filling her soul as her heart wanted to break in two.

Oh Lucy, please believe me?

25

Neither of them spoke for a few seconds. Then Lucy climbed out of her bed, sat beside Helen, and grasped her hand.

'I know how terrifying this whole thing must be for you. You've lost your husband in unusual circumstances and even if it wasn't a happy marriage, you were together for a long time.' Lucy squeezed Helen's fingers in hers and smiled at her. 'We both know you were not responsible for his death and I'm sure that once the detective hears your full story, he'll believe you.'

Helen's racing pulse slowed slightly. She drew a deep breath. 'I swear I had nothing to do with his accident. But I don't have an alibi for that missing hour or whatever it was when I was at the waterhole.' Aware of her rising tone, she sucked in another breath, swallowing her panic. 'What do you think will happen?'

Lucy hugged her. Outside, the bellow of a cow nearby reminded her of Elizabeth Downs. She searched for happier moments, but the image that came was always the same—the scene by the silos. The sun setting over her husband, crumpled on the ground and surrounded by members of the local fire brigade, a paramedic, and their employee, Warren. Sheets of iron from the dismantled silo lay scattered amongst the sorghum heaps and beside them was Jack's body, covered in red-brown dust, his face sallow in death.

'We had to pull the side of the silo off to get him out,' an emergency service officer had explained.

She'd remained mute, the shock rendering her immobile until the paramedic had taken her by the arm and gently guided her inside the house, away from the horrifying scene.

'I guess they'll go through everything with you again—and you can't really blame them. But if you tell them what you've told me, I'm sure there won't be a problem.' Lucy frowned. 'But it is puzzling. Do you really think someone may have pushed him?'

Helen shrugged. 'I don't know what to think. He borrowed money through a broker I've never heard of, so it crossed my mind there might be a creditor out there who's not happy. But if that was the case and they did pay him a visit, how come no one saw them? We might live out of town, but most farms were harvesting at the time so you'd think someone would have noticed any unusual vehicles. The dust trail gives visitors away.'

Lucy chuckled. 'True. Can't say I miss that—although during the occasional dry spell here, the air gets a bit dusty when we're sowing. Nothing like Australia though. Mud's more of an issue for us. Anyway, now that we're wide awake, how about another cup of tea?'

Her smile eased Helen's churning belly as she nodded and watched Lucy fill the kettle and pop the teabags in the mugs. As an only child with older parents, she'd grown up accustomed to her own company and had never felt alone. Her animals had been her friends. But since meeting Lucy and Roslyn at boarding school, the aura of true friendship had surprised her and now, a warm glow blossomed in her heart. Lucy really was a treasure, and Helen was pleased she'd come to Scotland to see her—even if it had been under a cloud.

'Tomorrow we'll visit the gardens then drive to Inverness, have a wander around the town, and stay in a gorgeous B and B I've organised,' Lucy said. 'The following morning we'll visit Culloden—a must, don't you think? Then we'll head back home so that you can rest up and get organised for your flight back to Australia. Okay?'

Helen nodded again as Lucy passed her the steaming mug. 'Sounds great.'

Half an hour later, as Helen drew the doona over her shoulders in the dark, her thoughts drifted to Michael.

He'll be arriving in Sydney any time now. I wonder what will be waiting for him—and if his situation will be any less complicated than mine.

For the hundredth time, she relived their chance meeting, their precious time spent together, and silently wished that somewhere in the near future their paths would cross again.

THE FOLLOWING day remained bright and sunny as they strolled around the stunning Inverewe Gardens before making their way to Inverness. A late lunch at a cosy café was followed by a visit to Leakey's Bookshop, the fascinating Scottish icon both women were loath to leave.

'I know we love books but there's more to see in this beautiful city.' Lucy spoke firmly, determined to show her friend the Scotland she'd become so fond of.

Helen laughed and they locked elbows, weaving up and down the paved walkways, admiring the architecture and exploring numerous shops. With small gifts for Lisa and her boys stowed in Helen's bag, they returned to the car and followed the GPS instructions to their B and B home overlooking the Moray Firth.

As the car crawled slowly up the tree-lined driveway, Helen released an involuntary gasp at the magnificent stone home, surrounded by colourful gardens.

'Gosh, how lucky are we to find somewhere so lovely—and close to Culloden at this time of year?' Helen exclaimed.

Lucy grinned. 'Sometimes it's handy to have family ties. This place belongs to a relation of Fergus's. He hadn't seen them for ages but a few years ago he caught up with them at a family funeral. They got along well and said any time we're over this way, they want us to make use of their guest house. So ... here we are.'

Half an hour later, ensconced in a tiny cottage tucked amongst trees in the garden, Lucy poured sparkling wine into two glasses and they sat in front of the cosy fire.

'This is really kind of you, Lucy,' Helen said. 'Our days are running out, but I've had a wonderful time—despite the unexpected hospital encounter. I hope it won't be the last.'

'Of course it won't,' Lucy laughed. 'It's been great being together—just you and me. Reminds me of that time Roslyn was called home from school when her grandmother died and you and I had a whole week in the boarding house because of the floods out west.

Remember we couldn't get home—and if we had, we may not have been able to get back? There were a few of us affected but being the eldest at the time, you and I were given privileges we didn't expect.'

They reminisced again over their teenage years—music night with the staff and other evenings where just the three of them played scrabble and watched movies. It had been then that Lucy had declared her desire to travel while Helen had revealed her obligation to her parents and their busy newsagency. Lucy's heart had broken when she'd realised how different their lives really were—her own loving, supportive family, animals, and the farm, compared with Helen's responsibilities to a tired family business and a life already planned for her.

She reached out and rested a hand on Helen's. 'I'm pleased we stayed in touch all these years—even if I've been a bit slack lately.'

Helen topped up their glasses and raised hers. 'To us—and whatever comes our way.'

Lucy blinked, then clinked her glass against Helen's. 'Whatever it is, we'll tackle it with a smile.'

Then she released a long, slow breath as Helen's hopeful brown eyes met hers.

———

26

A cold, silent house greeted Michael as he stepped through the doorway.

After dropping his bag on the floor, he switched on the lights and made his way to the kitchen where he pulled a water jug from the fridge and poured himself a glassful.

His body ached from sitting and his head swam from the lack of sleep.

I should be used to this by now.

Turning in a slow circle, he studied his surroundings. A stark, minimalistic room with polished tiled floors barely softened with leather sofas and an expensive entertainment unit. The only sign of habitation was a photo. It was of Michael and Nita with their two children, taken only months before Amy's death. It had been the final photo of the four of them and despite his heart breaking every time he studied it, Michael couldn't put it away. Anguish filled his veins.

She needn't have died. I might have saved her—if only I'd had the chance.

Dragging his gaze from the photo, he squinted, wishing the brightness away as he compared his sterile apartment to the cosy loch-side cottage on the Isle of Skye.

Off the lounge, wide, glass doors opened onto a balcony overlooking the harbour and beyond where twinkling lights shone in every direction.

His insides felt leaden, his chest even heavier as an ache filled his lungs.

Closing the blinds, he blanketed out the city and stood for a moment, drinking in his surrounds.

My house—one that feels less like a home than ever.

Later, having showered and unpacked, he sent a message to Julian.

Home safe and sound. Hope you're enjoying your last few days and the weather is kind? Love Dad.

He hit send and waited, conscious of the time difference between Sydney and Scotland. 'You're probably halfway up a hiking track somewhere,' he muttered.

Checking his phone again, he hesitated for only a moment and then sent a message to Helen.

Hi there. I'm back in Sydney and still alive. Hope that wrist isn't troubling you. Good luck with your trip home and everything that follows. He paused for a few moments, his finger almost touching the screen as he decided how to sign off. Then he added, *Michael* and a smiley face emoji.

Although it was almost midnight, he felt closeted, claustrophobic. He meandered around the tiny patio, consumed with memories and thoughts of his brief stay in Scotland while the hum of city night-life bustled below him. An hour later, with an empty stomach and a heavy heart, he trudged to the bedroom.

With the lawyer's meeting tomorrow, I need to get some sleep.

But it was the early hours of the morning before exhaustion took over and his eyelids finally closed, his head spinning with its burden of the upcoming day and a longing to be somewhere far, far away.

DULL WITH JET lag and sleep deprivation, Michael wove his way through the chaotic traffic the following morning. He'd experienced medical investigations before, but this was different. An aching sense of foreboding filled his insides this time. *With all medical positions, responsibility is key. I know that. But is this the one that spells change? Is it me "for whom the bell tolls"?* His shoulders sagged.

Jolting out of his reverie as a sharp toot of a car horn blasted behind him, he blinked at the green light, pressed his foot on the accelerator, and shot through the intersection.

GREG'S familiar lanky frame sat opposite Michael in the quiet room, its frosted glass walls hiding the identity of those walking past.

It had taken no more than a phone call from Scotland minutes after reading the initial email to reconnect with his old acquaintance from university days—now a respected lawyer.

They had discussed Amy's tragic death and Michael had forwarded the information he'd received. Greg had swiftly assessed the allegations and reassured Michael that it appeared Anita was grasping at straws.

But was she? He clenched his teeth in an effort to prevent his jaw from trembling.

'Sorry you had to cut your holiday short, mate,' Greg said.

Michael nodded, anxiously shuffling forward in his chair.

'As I said on the phone, this claim is a legal document and you have a right of reply,' Greg said. 'We'll prepare and serve your defence, then follow with the steps required in litigation—obtaining statements from others, documenting your version of the facts, collating hospital records of Amy's care et cetera. There will be a mention in court; a judge will check on the progress of the matter and confirm that legal steps are being complied with.'

'So will I have to appear in court?'

'Hopefully not. We are confident your ex-wife's allegations are misguided claims that will not be proven as negligence. There won't be a hearing unless the matter is unable to be settled through mediation.'

'Oh, I see.'

'If it is obvious there is no case, we will argue for the claim to be dismissed.'

'And what are the chances of that?'

'Let's just see what Anita's response is—via her legal team of course. It's possible she may be convinced to drop the claim but if she insists and forces the matter to hearing, the judge will decide.'

They discussed the process for a further few minutes before Greg closed the file and smiled at Michael. 'Now we've sorted the official stuff, tell me about your holiday. Did you enjoy Scotland?'

'Yes thanks.' Memories of the fresh green hills, wild rocky outcrops, and a gentle face highlighted by deep brown eyes tugged at him. In the sterile air-conditioned room, the Isle of Skye might have been on another planet. 'I'd like to go back.' Michael's throat felt scratchy. Dehydration. He needed a drink—something stronger than water.

As though reading his mind, Greg glanced at his watch and smiled again. 'Got time to join me for lunch? I reckon a beer would go down nicely.'

Michael allowed the shadow of a grin to touch his face as he pushed his chair back and rose to his feet. 'Sounds like a great idea.'

WITH DAYS TO spare before he officially returned to his duties, Michael stopped at the supermarket and replenished his food supplies on his way home. Then he tossed his dirty laundry into the machine, changed his clothes, and emptied the used boarding passes, notes, and assorted bits and pieces from his rucksack.

Although winter had arrived early, the sun shone, lifting the temperature and providing the perfect weather for outdoor activities. Reluctant to spend another second inside, Michael contemplated his next move.

Walking will help me think. It worked in Scotland, and it will work here.

It took only minutes to assemble a sandwich, fill water bottles, and return to his car with his pack slung over his shoulder.

'Garigal National Park, I think,' he said aloud, reassuring himself a brisk hike would stimulate not only his poor circulation after the long flight but his jumbled mind.

A short time later, coupled with his long, even strides, the fuzziness in his head began to clear. The mid-week day out of peak tourist season and school holidays provided a peaceful opportunity to think—and with the freshness of rural living and the unexpected bond he'd found in meeting Helen, Lucy, and their families, he explored his options.

Three hours later, the ripples of doubt that had woven its way through him melted away. He had changed. His whole life had changed, and a new world had opened up to him. There was a hurdle to get over first—Anita's allegations. Although the thought of it made his stomach curl, he was determined it would be resolved relatively quickly and not affect his long-term plans.

It was over to him to make changes—if he dared.

And he did.

27

———

It was her last day on Skye and as if to remind Helen of its beauty, the morning dawned clear and golden, and the heather glistened— its purple haze colouring the hillside behind the cottage. The breeze, too, had disappeared and the rain that had hovered the previous day was gone.

Helen and Lucy's sojourn onto the mainland had flown. Along with hordes of other tourists, she had enjoyed their morning at Culloden. With its fascinating but grim history, it had been easy to forget all that was facing her on her return to Australia. But weaving her way through crowds all trying to take photos without dozens of unknown others in them had been exhausting and both women had been grateful to return to the pretty little croft on the hill. And now her troubles returned as Helen began preparing for the flight home.

Lisa threw herself on her mother's bed, ignoring the clothes assembled in neat piles around the suitcase. She sighed heavily.

'That sounds like a moan,' Helen said.

'I can't believe our holiday is over. Julian and I've had such a great time. I hated saying goodbye to him.' Lisa's voice quavered, as if close to tears.

'I'm delighted that you got along so well—and managed to see and do so much in the short time you've known each other.'

Their eyes met and Helen raised an eyebrow.

It was not like Lisa to be like this. All her life her daughter had been the one to jolly her brothers—and parents—along when something wasn't going well. She was the vibrant one. The cheeky, organising girl who dealt with problems and laughed off criticism and negativity. Now this same woman's face was creased with despair.

'Has something gone wrong?' Helen asked gently.

Lisa shook her head and sat up. 'Nope. Just feeling sorry for myself.'

'Oh? Can you tell me why?'

'Because after all the weird, immature, and boring guys I've dated in the past, I've finally found someone who enjoys doing the same things I do, who's easy to talk to and is kind and understanding. We even both work in the animal care industry.' Her voice rose in pitch. 'How amazing is that!'

'And isn't that a good thing?' Helen frowned, confused that Lisa was allowing the positives to cloud her mood.

'It is ... but now we're heading back to Queensland and he's returning to Sydney before he begins his next locum—somewhere in outback New South Wales.'

A strange flutter in her stomach prevented Helen from answering immediately. She understood exactly what Lisa was saying—and was both embarrassed and stunned to admit she felt the same about Michael. *How ridiculous*, she chided herself. They'd known each other less than three weeks—a mere flash in the pan, especially after her husband's recent death. A stab of guilt wiped away her thoughts.

And you've got a whole raft of problems to wade through when you get home.

She met Lisa's gaze with an understanding smile.

'At least the two of you will be in the same country. Lucy and Fergus had thousands of kilometres between them to begin with—and so did Ingrid and Callum. But they made it work and are happy. Whatever is meant to be, will be. Not much point stressing over it now.' Helen swung her gaze back to her half-filled suitcase, hiding her fading smile from her daughter. *And the same goes for you*, she told herself briskly.

IT WAS a sorrowful farewell on the Armadale pier and the heavy clouds above them hovered, as though waiting for the chance to release a torrent of rain to remind them their holiday was over.

'I'll miss you,' Lucy said, squeezing Helen tightly.

'And I'll miss you … terribly,' Helen responded.

'It won't be long before I'm back in Queensland to be with Adam and Meg and the new little one. We'll catch up again then, hey?'

The women smiled at each other while fat drops splashed on their heads.

Lisa opened an umbrella and held it over them, fighting against the buffeting wind. 'They're about to load, Mum. Hop back in the car.'

With a final hug from Lucy, they dashed to the little black rental car and dived in.

While Lisa negotiated the vehicle onto the ferry's hold, Helen kept her head turned toward her beautiful, stoic friend. Gratitude filled her chest as she waved, uncertain if Lucy could see her through the now pelting rain.

Minutes later, the ferry chugged away from the pier, leaving Skye under a grey veil, obscuring the castle, and allowing an ache of sadness to form in Helen's heart. Her eyes prickled and, as the rain streamed down the windshield, she closed her lids and allowed the tears to trickle down her face.

They were going home. She didn't know what would be next and for a few seconds, she didn't care. Her time in Scotland had been like a dream—a fantasy. One that bore no resemblance to her real life in Australia. And with that thought sitting heavily in her heart, she pushed the memory of the detective's phone call aside and forced her thoughts to the possibility of finding a sweet country cottage surrounded by garden somewhere a long way from Elizabeth Downs.

28

Arriving at the gate of Elizabeth Downs evoked emotions that surprised Helen. As she parked outside the house, she sat in silence and stared.

Memories returned of their early years of farming —harvesting meagre crops during searing hot summers while the dread of pathetic beef prices kept her awake at night.

But it wasn't only the hardships endured over the years that returned to haunt her. It was the realisation that she had lived on this property, in this house, for her entire adult life—for longer than she had lived anywhere else. Visions of her children with their rosy cheeks and dusty clothes laughing as she piggy-backed them around the lawn, played hide-and-seek with them, and led them in never-ending circles on her old mare, drifted through her thoughts. She smiled. Those were the memories she must hold on to. The ones where she was happy.

Shaking her head in disbelief, she recalled the detective's words. "There is no confirmation of where you were?" Did they really believe she was a suspect? A murderer?

Her stomach churned again and bile rose in her throat. What was she to do? If no one had seen her sitting by the waterhole, and no one had seen her around the time of Jack's estimated death, what proof did she have that she wasn't at Elizabeth Downs?

She shivered, got out of the car, and hauled her suitcase from the boot, grateful for Tim's thoughtfulness. With Lisa having only one day after landing in Brisbane before she was expected to return to work, there was no chance of her driving Helen back to the farm. So Tim had booked Helen on a flight from Brisbane to Emerald and had left her car at the Emerald airport, enabling her to drive the remaining three hours home. She sighed.

The joys of living so far from the coast. But maybe not for much longer.

Her mind skipped to Jack again and a cold wave of nausea overtook her. Did they really consider his death as homicide? The coroner's report had ruled it as "Accidental Death" but there must have been something to make the police believe otherwise.

With a shudder, she picked up her bag and marched up the path to the door.

Inside, a bunch of bougainvillea filled a jar on the table, a note tucked under it. She picked it up and smiled.

Welcome home! I hope your holiday was everything you'd hoped it would be. Thanks for the photos. Chooks are happy and have been laying well, so fresh eggs, milk, and fruit are in the fridge together with a casserole for your dinner. I'll call tomorrow when you've had some sleep. Love Shelley.

Helen released a tired breath. The number of friends she had may be minimal, but they were gold to her. Lucy, Roslyn, and Shelley. With the exception of her children—and now perhaps Michael—those three women were the only people she believed she could trust.

29

———

etective Seal wasted no time after Helen had advised the police she was home, arriving at Elizabeth Downs at ten o'clock sharp the following morning.

He and his sergeant, Leanne, sat at the kitchen table, going over the events of the day Jack had died again and again.

'And you're quite sure of the times?' Seal said.

Helen nodded. 'Yes. I remember looking at the kitchen clock when I was asked to take Sally home. It was half past two and I'd just finished peeling the vegetables. It would have been less than half an hour before Sally and I left, and as she's around twenty minutes from town, I guess it would have been between three and three-thirty when I dropped her at her home. I didn't go in. She was sick and said she'd go straight to bed.'

'I see. Did you check the time when you got in the car?'

'No. I didn't think of it and didn't have my watch on. I never wear it to work because I have my hands in water so often. I remember approaching the track to the waterhole and thinking it was such a nice afternoon, I'd sit awhile and watch the birds.'

'Is that something you did often?'

'Not really. I'm generally too busy. On the days I wasn't at the restaurant or charity shop, I was working here or out in the paddocks.'

'So why did you stop on that particular day?'

She shrugged. 'I'm not really sure. I suppose because I could. Jack wasn't expecting me home until later and as he had Warren helping him, I didn't consider getting home as urgent.' Frustration was building inside her. She clamped her teeth together, wishing the interrogation over.

'So this ... diversion was random. A spur-of-the-moment decision.'

'Yes. I guess so.'

'And how long were you there?'

'I'm not exactly sure but I think about thirty or forty minutes. I don't think it would have been an hour. It was around four-thirty when I arrived home. I saw the ambulance and everyone near the grain shed so I ran over to see what was going on—and that's when Warren told me Jack was dead.' Her voice faded as the memory returned.

The two officers looked at each other, their neutral expressions giving nothing away while Helen's heart beat harder.

'Apart from Warren, is there anyone else who visits this farm? Anyone you think may have seen something?'

'Jack had people coming and going quite regularly. You know, produce trucks delivering fertiliser and seed. Sometimes the stock agent turned up and other times it was steel or sheet iron being delivered.'

She met the blank stare of the sergeant and elaborated.

'Jack and Warren have been building yards at the back of the farm—where it meets the scrubby land owned by a mining company. Jack had dreams of being a wealthy landowner.'

The moment the words were out, the sudden recollection of the shed kit Tim had discovered sprang to her mind. Was that something connected with those yards?

'And to your knowledge, was your husband expecting any deliveries on that day?'

She shook her head, focusing again on the detective's wrinkled face and his solemn, deadpan expression.

'None that I know of. He and Warren were concentrating on getting the sorghum off. They'd harvested one of the paddocks two days earlier and had it tested. The moisture content was perfect, so they wanted to keep going and get as much into the silo as possible, even though it was early in the season. We had good rain when it was planted so it was strong and matured earlier than in some years.'

A glazed look passed over the officer's face, as if he had no interest or understanding in growing crops. 'So definitely no other vehicles coming or going?'

While blowing out a slow breath, her eyes met his as she spoke clearly and concisely. 'I don't know. I wasn't here.'

'Thank you, Mrs Gooding. I appreciate your time and apologise for the inconvenience. We do have to be thorough and will let you know if there's anything more we need to discuss.'

Helen escorted them to their car, her arms folded against her chest.

Detective Seal pointed to the grain shed and silos. 'Do you mind if we take another look at the accident scene?'

'Not at all. Do you need me to come with you?'

He waved a dismissive hand. 'No. We'll be fine. Just want to double-check a couple of things.' Then, as the two of them strode toward the silos, he called back over his shoulder, 'Thank you again.'

Her head ached with worry and jet lag. Had her answers been enough? Was she still a suspect? Her insides churned as she wandered back inside the house, muttering to herself, 'If only this was all over. Having you lot crawling over the place doesn't look good for a sale.'

HELEN WAS LOADING the washing machine when the car drove away. She breathed a sigh of relief. *They obviously didn't find anything they needed to ask me about.*

Working mechanically, she dusted the furniture and vacuumed the floors, shocked at the number of spiders and other insects that had taken up residence in three short weeks. It was Monday and although she wanted to thank Shelley for looking after the chooks, her neighbour would be sleeping after working her regular Sunday night shift at the hospital. Helen understood how precious rest was and wouldn't dream of disturbing her.

So, she pulled on her boots and gloves and headed for the garden shed, determined to restore the place to its best before making the phone call.

An hour later, the ragged lawn was mowed and she had pulled a bucket of weeds from the vegetable garden.

'Here you go,' she said to the hens as she tossed the

greens into their pen. Then she checked their water and grain feeder, collected the eggs, and ambled back inside, wearing a satisfied grin. There was nothing more rewarding than spending time in the garden—except perhaps to be with friends. Her thoughts returned to the day they had all walked to the Point of Sleat. The smell of gentle waves washing over the untouched white sand came back to her while happy voices drifted around in her head. It had been the day she'd realised Michael had become more than the doctor who rescued her while out hiking.

An urge to ring him to ask how his meeting with the lawyer had gone had her reaching for her phone. But she pulled back at the last moment, withdrawing her hand as though the device was on fire.

No. If he wants you to know, he'll ring you.

A second later, the phone danced with an incoming call. Startled, her thoughts still on Michael, she took a few seconds before picking it up and swiping the icon. 'Hello, Shelley. You beat me to it. I thought you'd be sleeping.'

'I don't have to work tonight so I'll go to bed early. Tell me about the holiday?'

'It was great. But before I continue, thank you so much for checking on things here. And thanks for the fresh food and flowers.'

'You're welcome. How's your wrist? What happened?'

'Wrist is fine.' Helen flexed it as she spoke. 'I'm not supposed to lift anything heavy with it for a little while but it's not painful. The doctor did a great job.'

Then she proceeded to share the events of the hike and accident, leaving out only the surprisingly personal connection that had flourished between herself and Michael. Doubt still clouded her mind every time her thoughts drifted to him. Was she imagining something that wasn't real? Did he feel the same way she did—that whatever it was that had bonded them emotionally could possibly be more than a simple friendship? After the traumatic years living with Jack, she was still uncertain she wanted to encourage friendship with anyone, including Michael. But a tiny voice deep inside her head kept reminding her that not all men were like her deceased husband. She had to remember that.

'We ended up seeing him and his son, Julian, a few times as Lisa and Julian seemed to hit it off. I've never seen Lisa so despondent about leaving. She and Julian will be keeping in touch which is nice—you know how everyone seems to live on their phones these days.' She chuckled as she finished. Then, before Shelley could question her more, she switched focus. 'How's your harvest going?'

'Great thanks. Bill's been working ridiculous hours —as it always is when there's a crop to bring in. He did mention something that I thought I'd ask you though.'

'What is it?'

'Do you know anyone who drives a green Mercedes?'

'No. Why?' Helen's brow creased at the odd question. Who would bring a Mercedes to an area like this? She didn't think green was one of Mercedes' colours for a start, and with the gravel roads around the district, she wouldn't expect an expensive vehicle like that to appeal to anyone local.

'Bill saw it parked down a side street in town the other day. Then he remembered seeing one just like it when he was on the tractor in the paddock near where the road forks and turns toward your place. It was the speed of the car that caught his eye apparently. Heaps of dust so the driver must have been flying. He couldn't tell what type of car it was at the time but when he saw the one in town, he recognised it immediately. He thinks it might be one of those special paint jobs that people pay a fortune for. Anyway, it came out of your road and headed south.'

Helen's frown deepened. There wasn't much missed in a small rural area like theirs and anything other than the usual run-of-the-mill utes or four-wheel drives stood out. 'Does Bill remember what day that was?'

'When he saw it in town? Or when it was flying out of your road?'

'Our road.'

'I'll ask him when he gets in if you like.'

'Thanks. I've had the police here this morning. Or to be more precise, detectives.'

A sharp intake of breath sounded through the phone. 'Why?'

'Jack's death.'

'But they did all that questioning of neighbours and stuff weeks ago—before the funeral. What are they doing sniffing around again?'

'Because there seems to be a suggestion Jack's fall may not have been accidental. They questioned me very thoroughly. I'm not certain but I think they're considering me as a suspect.'

'What!'

Helen had to hold the phone away from her ear at Shelley's explosive yell.

'You mean they think you might have been there when the accident happened? Or ... do they really think you might have ... pushed him?'

'I don't know, Shelley,' Helen said tiredly. 'The whole thing seems preposterous to me. You know how rough-and-ready he always was—never took safety issues seriously and, knowing him, he would have been calculating how much money the crop would bring instead of watching where he put his feet.'

'I can imagine. Still, you don't need an investigation on top of everything else you've got going on.'

'I know. It might be worth letting the detectives know about that Mercedes though.'

'No worries.' She chuckled. 'Bill's not much of an observer but there must have been something about the vehicle that stuck in his mind. Probably just a tourist following their GPS and being led astray then getting so annoyed they tried to make up time.'

They both laughed and continued talking about Helen's holiday before ending the call almost half an hour later.

Helen made herself some lunch and had just sat down to eat when a vehicle approached, pulling to a halt outside the yard gate. She stood and pushed open the screen door, meeting Clint, the real estate agent's, beaming smile.

'Hello, Clint. I've just made a pot of tea. Like to join me?'

He nodded, tapping a finger on the folder he carried. 'Love to. I've got something here I think you'll be very relieved to see.'

30

———

*I*tching with excitement, Helen quickly grabbed a mug and poured the tea while Clint sat down and opened the folder.

'I know I'm being presumptuous but when you read this, I'm sure you'll agree I've done the right thing,' he said, his smile widening.

'What is it?'

'A contract for Elizabeth Downs.'

Helen had to grab the table as she slumped onto the chair, relief coursing through her. 'Anywhere close to our asking price?'

'Better,' he said, turning the document around and holding his finger on the offer amount. 'Two hundred thousand dollars more than even I dared to hope for.'

Their gazes met as Helen's veins fizzed. 'Really?' she squeaked.

'Yep. Prices are on the rise now and this family desperately want this particular property. Apparently, a relation of theirs lived and worked here decades ago —when Elizabeth Downs was hundreds of square miles and before the station was subdivided into smaller farms. Ironically, after having had no enquiries for a couple of weeks, I got two last Thursday and when I mentioned to these people that I was showing the property to someone else that morning, they made their offer "sight unseen".'

'Gosh. That's fabulous. Fancy wanting to buy it without even seeing it though.'

'Oh, they've seen it. They've driven past several times over the past year or so. I'm not sure why they haven't made enquiries earlier and I didn't ask. The main thing is that if you're agreeable to their offer, you now have a buyer—and a contract on Elizabeth Downs.'

Overwhelmed by a gamut of emotions—joy, relief, and panic—Helen's face paled.

After swallowing a mouthful of tea, her thoughts flicked to her earlier conversation with Shelley. 'Do these people drive a green Mercedes?'

Clint blinked, a puzzled look on his face. 'I don't know. I didn't ask what sort of vehicles they have. As they own a property near Biloela and another outside Emerald, I'd imagine they drive a four-wheel drive—or at least something suited to zipping back and forth between properties on back roads. Why?'

'It's nothing. A green Mercedes was spotted coming out of our road a while back and I was just wondering if it may have been them. Probably not though.'

He nodded and returned his gaze to the document, clearly dismissing Helen's comment as irrelevant. 'So ... thoughts?'

'Oh my goodness. Yes. Of course I'll accept their offer.' She beamed as the reality filtered through her. Not only would the burden of their debt be off her shoulders, but with the excess remaining after repaying the loans, she would be left with enough to purchase something for herself—even if it was small and a long way from the coast. She almost bounced on her chair with excitement.

'Fabulous.' He pulled a pen from his pocket and handed it to her. 'Happy to sign?'

She grinned and took it. Then, following his guidance, she read through the pages and signed her name as threads of hope wove their way through her.

Half an hour later, she waved goodbye to Clint then, hastening back inside, sent a group message to her three children.

As expected, Tim called within seconds, shortly followed by Steve and then finally, Lisa called soon after one o'clock while on her lunchbreak.

'Settlement will be in four weeks.' She repeated the

offer price and as many details as she could remember for each of her family before ending the calls.

Then she stood in front of the kitchen sink, staring through the window as she replayed the previous two hours over and over again. Her smile grew wider, her heart beat faster and, after glancing around her as if to ensure no one was watching, she clenched her fists and punched the air.

'Yes, yes, yes!' she hooted.

HELEN THOUGHT about it for another hour before her confidence strengthened enough to act. Then she selected Michael's number and tapped the green icon.

The phone rang, strident in the cool evening air. Once. Twice. Three times it repeated the familiar sound. As she dithered over whether to leave a message or cancel the call, he answered.

'Helen! How lovely to hear from you.'

'Hi, Michael. I hope this is not an inconvenient time?'

'Not at all. I'm sitting on my balcony having a coffee with nothing to do and nowhere to go.'

She chuckled, imagining his long legs stretched out in front of him as he stared out over the bustling city of Sydney.

'Great. Not at the hospital then.'

'No. I'm not … and I won't be again I hope.'

Dread swooped through her, chilling her core. Had something gone wrong?

'I'm so sorry to hear that, Michael. Is everything okay?'

'Yes. Don't worry. I've given my notice and it wasn't because of the issue I had to return home early for. It was my trip to Scotland.'

'Oh.' Helen wasn't certain what to say so she said nothing, hoping Michael would elaborate.

'My time over there—having Julian with me, being in that rugged and beautiful place, and meeting you and your friends—gave me a lot to think about. Then when I walked back into the hospital, I was shocked at my feelings.'

'In what way?'

'I realised I didn't want to be there—ever again.'

'Gosh. You poor thing. Are you saying you don't want to work in the hospital again or you don't want to be involved with medicine anymore?'

'I think it's just the hectic pace of the hospital, and while I know it doesn't matter where I work now—all Australian hospitals are busy—I think it has more to do with me feeling burnt out and admitting I need a change. So … I'm doing something about it.'

'Can you tell me what that might be?'

'I've applied for a couple of positions in small rural hospitals.'

'Oh! That's amazing. You don't think you'll be run off your feet just as much as in the big hospital?' She paused for a moment to absorb his news. It would be a huge change for someone who had lived in the city most of his life and could be disappointing.

But perhaps that's exactly what he needs?

'No. I was impressed with Broadford hospital, especially the more peaceful atmosphere, and while I understand rural hospitals and medical centres have their fair share of busy times, it won't be like it is here. I'm sure it will be a far more enjoyable workplace than rushing around here like a madman on steroids. I must be getting old,' he finished with a gentle laugh, and Helen joined in.

'Not old. Just sensible,' she said.

'Anyway, what's happening up your way? Any nibbles on the farm yet?' he asked.

She chuckled at his terminology. 'Yes—plenty of cattle nibbling the grass ... and a better one. I've accepted an offer for Elizabeth Downs and the contract has been signed. Settlement in four weeks.'

'That's fabulous. Congratulations. Will the offer cover the debts you spoke of?'

'Yes—and more. I'm so relieved. I'll have enough left over to buy something inexpensive, although most likely it will be in a less popular location than I'd initially hoped. But who knows, once I start looking around, I might be surprised.'

'Wonderful. And how's everything else going? Has the police investigation been finalised yet?'

A shot of fear stole her breath as the memory of the detective's interview returned. With the excitement of the sale contract, she had pushed it to the back of her mind, convincing herself she would receive a call any minute now confirming that Jack's death was accidental and the case would be closed. Sadly, that hadn't happened.

'No.' Her voice quavered. She cleared her throat and continued, 'They interviewed me again and inspected the "crime scene" as they called it. They seem sure that it was not an accident. I'm not certain if they believed me when I told them where I was. That's the problem with living in an isolated spot I suppose. While small country towns have more than their fair share of busybodies, living out here means not many people notice where you are or what you're doing.'

Shelley's revelation about the green Mercedes popped into her head. 'Actually, I take that back. Apparently, my neighbour saw an uncommon vehicle travelling at speed near our place the day Jack died. A green Mercedes.' She stopped abruptly, recalling the conversation she'd had with Shelley.

'Did your neighbour report the vehicle to the police?'

A silent pause dragged out between them before

Helen spoke in a low voice. 'We discussed it but I'm not sure. I'll ring them again and check.'

'Good idea. Anything's worth mentioning, even if it turns out to be nothing. But for your peace of mind, I hope the police do take note and at least investigate.'

'Thanks, Michael. I'll contact them now and let you know how we get on.'

'Please do. And I'll let you know if I hear anything from my applications.'

They said goodbye and ended the call, Michael's concerned tone heightening Helen's unease.

31

———————

The following morning, Helen stared at the phone before gingerly picking it up and tapping Shelley's phone number.

'Hello!' Shelley answered cheerily.

'Hi, Shelley. It's me, Helen.'

'I know. It doesn't sound like you though. Is anything wrong?'

'I'm not sure. You know the green Mercedes you mentioned? The one Bill saw the day Jack died?'

'Ye-es.'

'Have either of you mentioned it to the detective yet?'

'Oh no. I forgot about it.' There was a moment's pause. 'Is it urgent?'

'I don't know. I just think they should know—and

it's better to come from Bill as he's the one who noticed it.'

'Ok.' There was another pause while Shelley sucked in a breath. 'When the police called in here after Jack's death, they asked us if we'd been at your place that day or heard anything unusual. We hadn't, and at that stage, Bill hadn't mentioned the Mercedes.'

'And now?'

'Until he saw the car again last week, I don't think he'd given it a thought. But ... I wonder if it was someone visiting Jack while you were at work?'

'Hmm. Maybe. I'm sorry to put this on you, Shelley. But I'm so worried about being considered a murder suspect, I'm grasping at anything that might offer alternatives. Do you think Bill would mind ringing the police and letting them know what he saw?'

'Of course not.' Shelley's tone rose, the anxiety in her voice audible. 'He's in the shed mending an auger. I'll head straight over and let you know how we get on. Okay?'

'Thanks, Shelley. That would be great. It's probably nothing but you know what they say—even the slightest detail may help save a life. And in this case, I'm worried it might be mine!'

'Oh lordy. Surely it's nothing like that. I'm so sorry it slipped my mind. I'll let you know. Bye.' And with that, she hung up, leaving Helen staring at the phone again as she slumped onto a chair.

She slapped her forehead. *I forgot to tell her about the sale.*

WHILE WAITING for her friend's reply, Helen struggled to focus on anything, wandering aimlessly around the house and yard. The dry spell and winter frosts had burnt off much of the cattle feed and, wanting to ensure her stock were in prime health for the upcoming sale, she needed to take supplementary feed to them or shift them into fresh paddocks.

Glancing down at her mending wrist, she screwed up her face. Lifting anything heavy was not a good idea and she was reluctant to use the quad bike. But she had to do something—anything to take her mind off who owned the wretched green car.

She jammed her hat on and strode toward the machinery shed, relieved the tractor was already fitted with the forks for moving big round bales.

'Good on you, Bill. Thanks.' She smiled. Bill and Shelley were the best neighbours she could wish for— even if Shelley had forgotten to ask Bill to speak to the police about the Mercedes. Helpful and friendly, they'd never been intrusive or offered unwanted advice. Without ever having discussed it, Helen and Jack had formed the sort of neighbourly relationship with both Bill and Shelley that helped one another when asked but never stuck their noses in when not wanted. She would miss them.

Climbing into the seat, she made herself comfortable and reversed the tractor out of the shed. Then, after approaching the open hay barn, she shifted the lever to lower the forks, directed them into a bale, and carefully manipulated the lever again to lift the hay into the air. The slow drive across the wide yard and along the track to the most suitable fresh paddock for the cattle took ten minutes, the time dragging and feeling more like hours as she waited for Shelley's call.

It hadn't come by the time she had delivered three bales and parked the tractor back in the shed. So she studied the quad bike again and shook her head, speaking aloud.

'No. There's nothing wrong with my legs and a walk will be good for me.'

Then she strode along the track she had just driven until she reached the well-chewed paddock where more than a hundred head of cattle mooched about, their long tongues twisting around the last of the sorghum stalks and ripping them out of the dark soil.

Some began bellowing as she approached while others broke into a trot as they loomed toward her.

'Steady on, fellas!' she shouted. Glancing around before she opened the gate, she nodded with approval at the system she and Jack had set up years earlier—a central race wide enough for the farm equipment with all paddocks opening onto it. With careful operation of the gates, it allowed a single person to lock them open while the cattle took themselves down the lane and into the only other field open to them—in this case, the one Helen had delivered the hay to.

After the last beast galumphed past her, bucking and frisking at the knowledge of the smorgasbord up ahead, she chuckled, momentarily forgetting about Shelley's phone call.

The day passed slowly, the only interruption being the arrival of a telco truck whose passengers had been sent to maintain one of their systems and had taken the wrong road.

Pink and gold hues were appearing over the horizon before Helen's phone rang. She jumped, her heart racing as she scurried inside and fumbled with it.

'Shelley?'

'Yeah. Hi. Sorry it's taken me so long. You wouldn't believe it, the cops were super interested in that car. They asked so many questions.'

'Like what?'

'Oh—a detailed description of it, whether we'd ever seen it before. Did we know the number plate?' She grunted. 'As if. Bill only saw it whizz past. They were lucky he even recognised what sort of car it was. I wouldn't have had a clue—probably would have described it as a green car about the size of a Holden Commodore but it wasn't.'

They both giggled.

'I don't know what's next but after all their questions I'm beginning to wonder if someone else has commented on the Mercedes or come forward with something more. They certainly took interest anyway, so I don't think you should get too worried.'

A weight slid from Helen's shoulders as she absorbed Shelley's reassuring words. 'Thanks, Shelley. You're a gem—and I hope you're right.'

'I'm sure I am. Now ... what's happening with selling? I wasn't eavesdropping when we were in town, but I might have heard a whisper in the café that someone's made an offer on Elizabeth Downs.'

'I'm sorry. I should have told you that before. I've been so worried about being accused of murdering Jack—and that car—that I forgot to tell you the best news!'

'Don't be silly. For a start, you haven't been accused of anything. The detectives are simply wanting to put every little piece of the puzzle together before they start making arrests. So put that out of your head now and tell me what's happened!'

Without mentioning the exact amount offered, Helen shared the events of Clint's visit and the information he'd passed on about the new buyers. 'And the best part is the offer is more than I'd hoped for. I'll have enough left to buy something else—so I won't be homeless!' she squeaked with elation.

Shelley laughed again. 'I knew it would work out for you. You deserve the best and once this investigation is over, you'll be able to move forward and live the life you deserve.'

Her friend's words brought tears to Helen's eyes and for a few seconds, she struggled to speak. 'Thanks, Shelley.'

After ending the call, Helen remained on the kitchen chair, the air growing cold around her as the embers in the wood fire faded and died. The ticking of the clock remained the only sound as Helen painstakingly replayed the events of the day Jack died, the subsequent debt discovery and the current situation.

Eventually, she rose, rubbing her arms to warm them. It was very early to be going to bed, but she didn't care. She was exhausted, emotionally and physically, the long flight home still affecting her sleep patterns and the highs and lows of the previous days gruelling. So, she did a last check of the house, locking all the doors—something she had only started following Jack's death—and switched on her electric blanket.

Then she took a hot shower, made a mug of tea, and crawled under the cosy doona.

32

With a list of jobs to complete, Helen drove into town the following morning, advised the restaurant manager of her impending move and gave him her resignation. Then she collected a pile of empty boxes from the recycle bin behind the building and returned home to continue packing a lifetime of belongings.

Thanks to Lisa's assistance prior to their holiday, most of the work was straightforward. Steeling herself, Helen worked methodically, pausing only for a few minutes as she wrapped their collection of photos to reminisce over the happy times.

There had been some, she acknowledged, so she dwelt on them as she packed.

By the evening, she had finished all but her bedroom and the kitchen—and she resolved to leave them until the last week before settlement. Her main priority now was to decide where she would move to. Scrolling through the real estate websites on her laptop, she concentrated on the south-east corner of Queensland. She wasn't sure why that area appealed— only that she no longer wanted to live with long, hot summers, broken only by a few weeks of frosts and sporadic pleasant temperatures. After her visit to Scotland, she craved a climate that offered all four seasons. A place where autumn displayed its rich golden colours, where in winter the trees shed their leaves, and in spring she might be able to grow bulbs like some of those that grew wild on the Isle of Skye.

She was mulling over house sales in the Darling Downs and Granite Belt areas when the phone rang, startling her.

'Hello?'

'Helen. It's me, Lucy.'

Helen smiled at the sound of her friend's cheery voice. She'd been home barely a week and despite all that had happened in that short time, had missed Lucy's comforting presence.

'Hi, Lucy. How're things on sunny Skye?'

'Huh. Not so sunny since you left. It's rained for four days straight and now the temperature has dropped it feels as though we're back in autumn again.'

Helen laughed, remembering the sudden turns of Skye's summer days into what felt like a Queensland mid-winter—all in one day. 'How's Fergus? And everyone else.'

'Everybody's fine—and I have some good news. I've booked my flights. I'll be on Binnalong in a little over three weeks. It's still a month before the baby's due but I thought I might come up and spend some time with you at Elizabeth Downs?'

'Oh, Lucy. That would have been wonderful. But I've accepted an offer on the farm and the contract has been signed. I have less than four weeks before settlement.'

'That's fabulous news!' Lucy almost shouted, forcing Helen to pull the phone away from her ear as a grin spread across her face.

'Yes. Fantastic. Only now I'm in a real quandary. I don't know where to go.'

'Is there a hurry? I mean—could you rent something for a little while until you've had a good look around?'

A crease formed between Helen's eyes as she thought about Lucy's suggestion. It would be a good option—if she could find something suitable. With the current housing shortage, any vacant dwelling was hard to find whether for sale or rent and she had never rented a house in her life. What would her chances be?

She voiced her concerns to Lucy, and they discussed options for several minutes.

'So that's settled then,' Lucy said firmly. 'You'll join

me on Binnalong for a little while. I'll stay in the house with Adam and Meg, and you can have my wee cottage. If Meg's well enough, perhaps you and I could have a couple of days browsing around some of the areas you're considering moving to. We could stay with Vonnie, Ingrid's mum, in Toowoomba and scout around from there. It'll be fun—and a wonderful chance to spend more time together again before the baby comes.'

Helen smiled as a cloak of peace rested on her shoulders.

FIZZING WITH EXCITEMENT, Lisa wished the time would pass more quickly. Julian's text less than an hour earlier had provoked her curiosity and filled her with hope.

Received my new posting. Coming your way. Ring me in your lunchbreak.

In the week since they'd returned to Australia, they had exchanged more emails and messages than Lisa could count, every one of them warm with friendship, memories, anticipation and something a little more— was it early love? Now optimism filled her soul and heightened her already energetic body.

Back in the surgery, her workload had been hectic, her days filled with the usual medical procedures plus a run of accidents involving wildlife. As the most experienced native animal vet nurse in the practice, the responsibility of caring for a koala with multiple injuries after being hit by a car and a wallaby with a broken arm, also the result of a road accident, weighed heavily on her. A staff shortage added to the pressure as, with winter's arrival, a round of influenza viruses had descended, progressively keeping many of the staff at home. So, lunchbreaks had become short, if they came at all.

'All done,' Stuart, the vet announced, gently wiping the perfectly sutured wound on the labrador's belly with a gauze wipe. 'Next?'

Lisa gathered the dog into her arms as Chrissie, another of the nurses, lifted a drowsy Cavoodle onto the operating table. 'Last one,' she said.

Glancing at the clock, the butterflies took flight in Lisa's stomach. 'Are you right if I take a quick break now?'

'Fine by me,' Chrissie said.

'Sure,' Stuart added. 'I'll have lunch after this one then will be back by two for afternoon consultations.'

Lisa shot them both a smile, pushing the door open with her back and then laying the labrador in a large cage on the floor.

She grabbed her bag and darted outside, hurrying to the picnic table under a tree in the yard—a popular spot for staff breaks. Then she swiped her phone and tapped Julian's name.

'Hi there!' His voice sounded higher than normal, widening Lisa's grin.

'Hi to you too. What's news?'

'I'm coming to Queensland.'

'Really?'

'Yep really. Not exactly next-door neighbours though. I've scored a locum in a practice somewhere inland from the Gold Coast. A town called Beaudesert.'

The initial spike of joy faded a little when he announced the town's name. Although in Queensland, Julian would still be more than a two-hour drive away. She blinked, sparking up again. 'Oh, that's wonderful.'

Compared with the drive to and from Elizabeth Downs, two hours would be a doddle—and at least they'd be a lot closer than if he was in New South Wales or anywhere else in Australia.

'Sure is. We'll be able to see each other regularly— and I'll be working with horses. Something I really wanted to do.'

'I'm pleased for you.' She hesitated for a moment, considering all they'd discussed in the past month. They hadn't talked about horses. A soft smile hovered on her face. *Probably too busy enjoying each other's company—in other ways.* 'Have you had much to do with horses?'

'Quite a lot at the last place I was working, but other than that only when Amy and I were kids. She was horse-mad for a while, so Mum organised riding lessons for us both. I can't say I was thrilled with the idea at first —all I wanted at the time was to race motorbikes. But I never could say no to Amy, and she thought she was the bees knees riding with her handsome big brother. All her little riding school friends were jealous apparently.'

He hooted with laughter, and she joined in.

'So modest too.' Still grinning, her thoughts switched to the horses her own workplace cared for. Not only were there racing stables nearby but several dressage and show-jumping clients, including two she had gotten to know well. 'Beaudesert's a big horsey area, so you'll be busy I expect. When do you start?'

'Next week.'

Her mind raced. With nothing planned over the weekend once the Saturday morning consultations were over, she had considered having a lazy time, completing her unpacking from the Scottish trip and catching up with her favourite shows on television. But if Julian was going to be so close, perhaps ...?

'Will you be here over the weekend?'

'Tomorrow, I hope—but not until late. There's a small cabin in the grounds of the surgery apparently. Nick—that's the vet's name—said a couple of his locums have used it but others rent elsewhere. He warned me it wasn't exactly palatial. So I thought if I got on the road first thing in the morning, I'll have Sunday to check it out and if it's okay, I'll move in.'

'Sounds wonderful. Do you know what days you'll have off?'

'Not yet. There are two other vets apparently, including Nick, four nurses, and a receptionist. I'll be expected to be on the emergencies roster, and he did say some weekends can be busy as that's when most equestrian events are held.'

Determined not to let disappointment squash her hopes, Lisa took a deep breath. 'That sounds fabulous. Maybe once you've settled in and know what days off you're likely to have, we could see each other?'

His voice softened, and there was a smile in his tone when he said, 'My thoughts exactly. When I was accepted by both the Scone practice and this one, the first thing I did was work out how long it would take to drive to see you—and of course Beaudesert won.'

They talked for another few minutes as Lisa shared the news of the farm's sale, before Chrissy threw open the back door and called out. 'Can you come in please, Lisa? We've got an emergency.'

'I've gotta go,' she said, rewrapping her uneaten sandwich and grabbing her drink bottle. 'Talk again later?'

'Sure. I'll ring after dinner.'

'Thanks,' she whispered. Then she slipped her phone inside her pocket and hurried into the surgery.

33

Filled with elation, Lisa spent an hour talking to her mother after finishing a lengthy call with Julian later that night, sharing Julian's latest news and her hopes that they would soon be able to see one another on a regular basis.

After the negative memories of Elizabeth Downs—her father's temper, the long, hot summers that seemed to bake everyone's moods to a crisp, and the alternating droughts and floods that plagued inland Queensland—Lisa felt as though at last the page was turning. Her mother would be free to begin a new life. Her brothers had already made theirs—and she supposed she had too really. Only, as long as her mother lived on the farm, she could never leave it completely.

'I'd like to come and help you, Mum. I'd organised

an extra day off work so Julian and I could catch up but now he has to work that weekend. So if nothing unexpected happens, I'll leave here before daylight on the last Saturday before settlement. Then I'll return on Monday. That'll give us Sunday to finish whatever's left to do and have a final drive around the farm.'

'Great idea,' Helen said. 'Shelley and Bill have been over and taken most of the stuff to store in their shed for me. There's not much left and what there is should fit in my car.'

'What's happening with the police investigation?'

Helen blew out a long breath. 'I haven't seen the detectives since they came and interviewed me. The last I heard was that Bill told them about a strange vehicle he saw near our place on the afternoon your father died.'

'So you're no longer under suspicion?' Lisa spoke cautiously, almost afraid to ask.

'I can't be. Nor am I worried any more. If they thought I was responsible for your father's death, I'm quite sure they would have arrested me by now. I know where I was and what I was doing that day.'

Lisa raised her eyebrows at her mother's brisk tone. It was understandable she was angry. Even the suggestion she'd had anything to do with her father's death was preposterous. She shrugged. *I suppose they were doing their job.* 'Shame they ruined your holiday.'

'I know. But Lucy's coming home in a couple of

weeks and I'm going to stay with her while we check out what's available in real estate.'

Their conversation continued until Helen had provided answers to every one of Lisa's questions.

She lay back on her bed, her phone beside her, and smiled.

I've waited so long for this. I'll have both my mother and a gorgeous new boyfriend within a couple of hours' drive of here. Not quite perfect but a great start.

In the stillness of Elizabeth Downs main bedroom, Helen snuggled into bed, warmed by the electric blanket—comforted by the exhilarating conviction that her future was already taking a brighter turn.

Though parting from the farm brought its share of heartache, it was the flashes of happiness—moments that felt like gifts rather than grief—that stayed with her. And with quiet resolve, she leaned on the truth she had always believed: good things come to those who wait.

The following weeks passed quickly as Helen completed her packing, negotiated a fair price with the new buyers for the cattle, and watched the most valuable of the farm equipment being driven or trucked away. The middle-aged stock agent who had been advising Helen and Jack for years, together with umpteen phone calls to and from Tim and Steve, had ensured the steady procession of departing vehicles emptied the farm sheds while the bank balance steadily rose—*temporarily*.

Helen stood by, expressionless, as the final tractor—the massive green one that had been the catalyst in their farming venture—was driven down the lane. It had been purchased by a near neighbour, and Helen couldn't bear to watch the smug expression on the man's face as he climbed into the cab. She turned away and hurried to the chicken coop.

'I'm glad you girls will be living at Shelley's place,' she said to the russet-coloured hens clucking around her feet. 'Thank you for giving me so many eggs.'

As ridiculous as it sounded even to her own ears, a lump formed in Helen's throat. There had always been hens on Elizabeth Downs—and she was certain there would be again. With no dog and, after another day, no chooks either, piece by piece, the home she'd lived in for the majority of her life would no longer be hers.

Suddenly, the urge to leave, to get away from not only the farm but the entire district, had her almost running into the house.

After snatching up her laptop, she waited until the

wi-fi connected then began scrolling through the pages of real estate.

It was as she trawled through the houses for sale on the Darling Downs and Granite Belt that she remembered the unexplained materials for what Tim had revealed as a shed. She hadn't seen it leave the property on the back of a truck and had meant to ask the boys who had bought it. Unsure why the need to check on it had become so urgent, she closed the laptop again and hurried to the old shed, relieved the yard was now devoid of hungry buyers and agents. Turning away from the now empty buildings, she slipped behind the row of casuarina trees she'd planted twenty years earlier and approached a timber-slatted building standing alone and forlorn. Its rusted roof sagged under the weight of casuarina needles. Hidden behind the rear of the much newer machinery shed, the old building was anonymous in its solitude, its heavy doors held awkwardly by steel, farrier-crafted hinges.

It took several minutes to heave the doors open while protecting her wrist as much as possible. Eventually, light streamed into the cobweb-filled shed and she stared at the tarpaulin-covered pile in the corner.

It was still there.

She pulled her phone from her pocket and tapped Tim's number.

'Hey there, Mum.'

'Hi.' Something flew past her ear, and she jumped. 'Whoa!'

'What is it?'

She shook her head and grinned. 'I'm standing at the door of the old shed and a bat just flew past me.'

He chuckled. 'Could be worse I guess.'

'Yuk', Helen said, conjuring up visions of rats, fleeing possums, or worse—a massive king brown snake. 'True. I was thinking about that shed kit you spoke about when I was in hospital. It's still here.'

'Ahh. Sorry, Mum. Forgot to let you know I called our normal suppliers, but no one knew anything about it. And when I talked to the accountant, he said there was no mention of the purchase in either the current year or last year's books. I meant to ask you about it when you got home but ...' He trailed off and drew a noisy breath. 'I've been busy shifting cattle back into the north now the wet season's over.'

'It's okay, love. It probably doesn't matter anyway. Looks like the new owners have scored themselves a shed—if they care to erect it.'

'Okay. It could be worth a few grand. I counted the sheets and pillars and reckon it's about the size of a standard double garage—but judging by the posts, it's higher than normal. Why don't you put it on the community page and see if you can sell it? You never know—whatever you get for it could be the difference between buying a house in a not-so-nice street to buying somewhere more suitable?'

She sighed. Trading anything other than farm stock had never been her forte. Besides, she knew nothing about sheds—except they cost more than you expected and took a surprising amount of skill to erect correctly. 'Okay. I'll talk to Bill and see what we can do. Only have a week left and then you'll all be here to say a final goodbye to Elizabeth Downs. Then I'm going to Roma to stay with Lucy.'

'Great. I'm not sure I can make it back before the settlement though. Sorry.'

There was something in Tim's voice that triggered a deep sadness inside her. He felt it too. The end of an era. A final farewell to all they'd been through. She suspected he didn't want to return—and she didn't blame him.

'I understand. You've done a great job helping with the dispatch of the equipment and tractors, and I know how busy you are at this time of year. Talk again soon, hey?'

'Yep. Love you, Mum.'

'Love you too.'

She ended the call and stared into the shed. Yes, it was the end of an era. But there was so much to look forward to—and so much she would never have to repeat.

I'm not sorry to be leaving.

34

'Not a problem,' Bill said. 'I've been considering putting up another shed so this will save me going through the research. 'I'll give you a fair price and come and take it this afternoon if that suits?'

Helen sagged with relief. She didn't care how much Bill paid her—anything was better than nothing and she trusted his judgement.

She cast her gaze around the almost-empty kitchen. Gone was the clutter that regularly sat on the end of the counter until someone—usually her—found a home for it or threw it away. There were no vases on the windowsill filled with bunches of parsley or posies of wildflowers, no electric gadgets that had been used so regularly it seemed pointless putting them in a cupboard, and no dishes sitting in the drying rack. All that was left was the tea and coffee caddies, two mugs, and a calendar on the wall—a reminder of the days left on Elizabeth Downs.

With the exception of bird calls outside, the farm was quiet. The cattle had been moved again to a paddock well away from the house before the clearing sale, there was no drone of tractors or other implements, and even the windmill had clanked to a stop in the still air.

Swallowing the lump in her throat, Helen grabbed her hat and a bottle of water before heading outside. The air was crisp, the day bright and still. Above her, a few lazy clouds drifted by, the only sign of movement besides her steady steps.

The farm was almost seven thousand acres and dismissing the years of drought and flood, Helen reflected on the positives. In a good season, it had been enough to generate a living from and if they had managed it better, it should have carried them through a bad year or two. But alas, that hadn't always been the case.

Perhaps if I'd known more or helped more when the children were little, things might have been different?

Then she shook her head knowingly. A successful business needed a good team to succeed—and that had been their downfall. In practical terms, they had been neither a team nor a partnership.

Lisa had said they would take a drive around the

boundary before the new owners arrived, but in case something cropped up and, like Tim, she decided not to come, Helen had an urge to walk over her favourite part of the farm to remind herself of what she and the creditors owned—if only for a few more days.

It took longer than she remembered but she enjoyed the walk, her thoughts constantly on the past.

The quad bike had been handy for zipping out to check water and feed, or to mend a broken fence. Her beautiful mare, too, had made riding the boundaries checking for problems or evidence of predators easy, but somewhere over the previous few years, that had become Jack's domain. She hadn't minded. Her part-time jobs and the vegetable garden had kept her busy. There had been years when she reared motherless calves too. She smiled as she recalled their pretty faces as they waited impatiently, bellowing for their morning and evening milk.

She paused as she reached the top of a rise and took another mouthful of water. A sudden buzzing in her back pocket made her jump. After removing her phone and glancing at the screen, she grimaced. Private number.

'Hello?'

'Mrs Gooding. Detective Seal.'

Her heart leaped. Did this mean good news? 'Hello.'

'We've had another chat with your ex-employee, Warren Peck.'

'Oh yes.'

'At this stage, there's no evidence he's responsible for your husband's death although it's clear he has information that he's not prepared to share—not yet anyway.'

'So ... are you saying Jack's death was an accident after all?'

'It seems likely. However, we're following several lines of enquiry. I have your number and will keep in touch.'

'Oh! Thank you.' Her head filled with questions, but she said nothing as butterflies swirled inside her. 'I'd appreciate that. I'm leaving on Friday. That's when the new owners take over. You have my number.'

'Thank you, Mrs Gooding. You're free to go.'

Helen stemmed the giggle that threatened, feeling more like a student released from detention than a mature-aged woman who, until now it seemed, had been a suspect in her husband's murder.

Slipping her phone back into her pocket, she took a final sweeping gaze around her, conceded the distance she'd walked was enough for the day, and turned for the homestead.

BILL AND SHELLEY arrived that afternoon to collect the shed kit, leaving a copy of the bank transaction and a delicious chicken curry in a pretty casserole dish.

'I had a feeling you wouldn't be bothering to cook much for yourself, and I couldn't resist this gorgeous container. The perfect size for you and perhaps one other.' She shot Helen a friendly wink and they both laughed.

'I admit I've been living on bits and pieces left in the fridge and freezer. Can't see much point in buying anything now—so last night's dinner was an onion, three sausages I found in the bottom of the freezer, and a can of tomatoes. Breakfast was eggs—of course—and a handful of steamed greens from the garden.' She sighed. 'It turns out none of the kids are able to come home for a farewell visit so I didn't bother shopping, especially after Clint sent me a message to ask if the buyers could bring the settlement day forward so they've got the weekend to move in. I agreed.' She shrugged. 'Nothing left to stay for really.'

'I thought that might happen. So on Thursday night you're joining us for dinner.'

Helen smiled at her neighbour's no-nonsense command and nodded. 'Alright. By then I really will be down to an empty fridge and a few tins in the cupboard, so I'll accept. Thank you.'

She hugged Shelley and waved them goodbye as a surge of gratitude stirred within her. Then she re-entered the empty house and returned to her laptop to search through the real estate sales. She navigated to the area she'd decided appealed to her the most—the Darling Downs and Granite Belt or, more specifically, Stanthorpe—and scrolled slowly through.

An hour later, as the evening chill crept over the old house, she showered and warmed Shelley's curry. After eating dinner and washing her meagre utensils, she curled up in front of the fire with a blanket around her and studied the list she'd made.

Ten of the properties for sale intrigued her, so she listed the addresses and links on a notepad. Some were out of her price range but might be worth taking a look at for comparison. Others looked liveable and were within budget—but were they the product of clever photography? She shrugged. They might indicate what the market price entailed and whether or not her hopes were nothing more than dreams.

She picked up her phone.

Lucy will know more than me about what's worth looking at and what's not.

35

A thousand kilometres away, Lisa and Julian sat shoulder to shoulder on the tiny sofa in the cabin behind the Beaudesert Veterinary Practice.

Julian kissed her lightly on the forehead, pushed himself to his feet, and crossed the floor in two strides to fill the kettle.

'So you're happy you've made the right decision?' Lisa asked.

He flicked the switch and sat down again, wrapping his arm around her shoulders and pulling her to him.

'Yep. I love it here. Especially with you in my life. I don't think I've ever been happier.'

Tears of joy prickled the backs of Lisa's eyes. She blinked and hugged him. It was the first time she'd visited and was surprised how at home she felt. The cabin was clean and smelled of wood smoke, fried steak and onions, and a touch of aftershave. In front of the pot-bellied stove, a black and tan kelpie dog lay on a folded blanket, its back leg encased in plaster.

She pointed to the dog. 'And now you have Bobbie.'

'Yes. Poor boy. Not microchipped and no one has a clue where he's from. Certainly not local anyway.'

'Will you keep him?'

'I hope so. No one else wants him—nobody responded to the notices we put up, and the only inquiries we got from the social media posts were people without proof of ownership and who I suspect just wanted a free dog.'

'What about the other staff?'

'They've all got their own menagerie, so I'm the best chance he's got.' Julian slipped off the sofa and knelt beside the dog whose tail thumped the floor in delight while Julian stroked his head. 'He's friendly enough—and now he's desexed, any wandering he's been doing should come to a halt.'

'Maybe that's how he's survived this long? Wandering. Getting food wherever he could and secretly hoping that one day he'd find someone who loves him.'

Julian's blue eyes met hers, their edges crinkled with amusement. 'Like me you mean.'

Lisa laughed, dropping to her knees beside him and kissing him on the cheek. 'If the shoe fits ...'

His head turned and their lips met, gently at first,

then more intense as heat rose inside her. Their kisses deepened. Minutes later, Lisa pulled back, wonder filling her eyes as they met his.

Then gently, slowly, and without a word spoken, they rose to their feet, crossed to the bed on the other side of the room, and fell onto the soft, featherdown doona, wrapped in each other's arms.

IN SYDNEY, Michael sighed with relief as he read the words that allowed him to move forward. Skimming over the claim that "You did not act appropriately to save your daughter", his shoulders sagged at the final sentence "Claim has been dismissed".

He flopped back in his chair and stared at Greg. 'You're one in a million. Thank you.'

'It's my job,' Greg said, his head held high. 'And I strive for fairness and justice. It was fortunate there were so many witnesses the day of Amy's death. You followed protocol and left the room, which was the correct thing to do. Thankfully Anita's legal team were able to get that through to her. Things could have got a lot more stressful if they hadn't been able to convince her.'

'Yes. I realise that. I'm not sure what suddenly made her do this—blaming me for not treating Amy when she knew I was not able to?'

'It could be anything. Someone with influence over her but little knowledge—perhaps a friend or new partner? But whatever goaded her into having a final dig at you failed.'

Michael shook Greg's hand before they edged toward the door.

'Good luck with your new life, mate. I'm sure it will go well and if you're back this way, give me a call.'

'I will. Thanks again. I'll sort out the bill on the way out and hopefully, our next get-together will have nothing to do with claims, allegations, or ex-wives.'

Greg chuckled. 'Take care.'

'I will.' As he walked down the corridor to reception, the drawn, anxious expression that had lived on Michael's face for weeks morphed into a wide smile that deepened the wrinkles around his eyes.

DAYS LATER, Michael handed his apartment keys to the tall, slender woman with Botox-enhanced lips and false eyelashes. *What's with these pretty girls who're afraid of being natural?* He returned her artificial smile and nodded.

'I expect a call if you have any questions—and of course look forward to receiving the quarterly reports you mentioned.'

She acknowledged him with another false smile,

and he turned and walked out of the real estate agency office.

He slid into the car, rested his hands on the steering wheel, and released a slow breath.

What a week. No, make that a month!

The hospital farewell had been brief, but he'd been surprised to see old faces he'd worked with years earlier. It had left an odd feeling inside him. Not regret—he'd made the right decision to make changes to his life. It had been more of a sadness. For so long, he'd put his department, the patients, his fellow colleagues, and his career first. In doing so, he'd lost his daughter, his marriage—and his way.

Straightening his shoulders, he pushed the ignition button and fastened his seatbelt.

No more. This is my chance for new beginnings and I'm not going to stuff it up again.

Then he nudged his way into the stream of traffic and headed north, the sudden desperation to leave his previous, over-dedicated life behind him urging him on.

ON THE SAME DAY, in central Queensland, Helen added an esky full of treats and leftovers to her already loaded car, courtesy of Shelley from the previous night's dinner.

Then she drove slowly down the rough track, adrenaline racing through her as she left Elizabeth Downs behind. Although the journey to Binnalong would take only six hours, it had been so long since Helen had driven anywhere for pleasure, she'd decided to allow two days, staying at an inexpensive motel en route—perhaps Rolleston. She would stop and take in the scenery, visit the information centre in the little towns she passed through—if they had one—and perhaps wander around and study the birdlife and local architecture. The following morning, she would detour from the main road and enjoy a short walk in the Carnarvon National Park, a destination she had always wanted to visit.

Her chest tightened as excitement rose. Within half an hour, she was cruising southwards with a smile on her face and the sweet voice of Olivia Newton John pouring from the car radio.

She didn't look back, focusing on the road ahead while she sang along to the music.

Kilometres passed as the winter sun rose, and all the way, visions of the perfect country cottage surrounded by flowers circled in her mind.

36

Helen's arrival at Binnalong was greeted by the barking of excited dogs, Lucy's bear hug, and both Meg and Adam's enthusiastic welcome.

She had enjoyed her deviation into the national park and had walked for over an hour before continuing on her journey. The break had been restorative and enlightening and the trail surprisingly busy, mostly with retirees exploring inland Queensland while the weather was pleasant. She had talked with more friendly faces than she remembered meeting since her school days.

When she'd finished lunch and was back on the road to Binnalong, the ache to see her friend had again grown. She'd switched on the cruise control, knowing she'd be tempted to drive too fast as a whole new excitement filled her soul.

'Come and see where you're staying first,' Lucy said. 'Then I'll show you around before the sun sets and we join Adam and Meg for dinner.'

Lucy tucked her arm into the crook of Helen's elbow and led her friend toward the cute, timber-clad building on the far side of the farmyard.

When Helen stepped inside, she released an audible sigh of content. 'This is gorgeous, Lucy.'

'Isn't it? Despite being only one bedroom. Dad built it years ago and lived here after Robert and I married. Then when he and Robert were killed in the accident, I only used it for the occasional worker in the busy season. Meg came to live with us a couple of years ago and I felt they needed their privacy. So ... I cleaned this up, refurbished it to my tastes, and it became my little den. I stay here when I come back—not that I'm staying here as often as I originally thought I might. I love Skye—and Fergus too much. Anyway, it's yours now for as long as you need it. Adam and Meg are quite happy to have me in the house with them.' She smiled and leaned close to Helen. 'I actually think they want me there in case Meg goes into labour during the night.'

'I get it. How long has she got now?'

'Officially two weeks but you know what it's like. Things can happen whenever they're ready.'

Helen frowned. 'Are you sure you can spare time for us to go house hunting?'

Lucy flapped a dismissive hand. 'Of course. We'll do it in stages. Have a day or two here for you to get to know the place, then we'll nip into Toowoomba for a couple of nights. I know it's four hours away but from there we can explore areas like Crow's Nest, north of the city, and nip down to Warwick and Stanthorpe for a day trip. It will be a big day but if we're organised, we can at least look at some of the houses you've selected. Then we can come home to think things over and if you want to return and spend time in a particular area to get a feel for it, you can—and I'll stay here. What do you think?'

Helen chuckled. 'You certainly are an organiser, Lucy. Thank you. That would be really nice and having you with me will be fabulous.' She shrugged. 'I've never bought a house in my life—as you know, when you buy a farm, you get whatever dwellings are on the property unless you have the money to build something new.'

'Of course. But this time you can choose and even if it needs some work or tidying up, it's still yours.' Lucy gestured toward the homestead. 'I'll leave you to unpack while I pick some vegetables for tonight's dinner. Come over to the house when you're ready.'

Helen smiled as Lucy swept out the door.

An hour later, Helen sat opposite Meg at the Binnalong dining table, inhaling the delicious scent of the Thai chicken dish that Lucy had whipped up in a surprisingly short time.

'It's all about marinating the meat early,' Lucy said when Helen commented on the speed at which the meal had been prepared. 'I always think the slowest job in cooking any stir fry is preparing the vegetables.'

Across the table, Meg nodded. 'And when you're heavily pregnant, standing for ages chopping isn't my favourite pastime. Love ya, Lucy. You're a gem.'

The young woman's smile lit her round face, though the dark smudges beneath her blue eyes hinted at tiredness. She flicked her chocolate-brown hair from her shoulders and leaned forward, fork in hand.

'Not long to go now, Meg,' Helen said, her voice sympathetic. It was clear the girl was struggling with the final stage of her pregnancy and for a few moments, guilt penetrated Helen's stomach. 'Will you be alright if Lucy and I are away for two or three days?'

Adam lay his hand on Meg's. 'She's got me, and I've promised I won't go anywhere without her. And if I do—like to check cattle—she'll be coming with me.'

Their eyes met and she nodded in agreement. Their love for one another shone, warming the air around her. Helen's face softened.

They whiled away the evening watching a movie before first Meg and then Helen conceded defeat and said goodnight.

Lucy linked arms with Helen's as they crossed the yard to the cabin.

Above them, a full moon shone brightly, its silver glow illuminating the buildings and highlighting the deep crimson of the bougainvillea. Somewhere in the night, a boobook owl hooted.

'I love this time of day. Don't you?' Lucy said.

'Yes. It's peaceful and yet when you stop to listen, you hear life everywhere. That's what I like most about living in the country—no roaring vehicles up and down the road and no sirens screaming.'

'Are you sure you want to live in a town—even a small one?' Lucy asked.

Helen shrugged. 'It's a matter of practicality. I know my budget won't buy me the ideal acreage I would love, even if small. But I'm hoping I'll find something close to my heart. Something that might be a compromise but that speaks to me.'

'I'm sure we'll find what you want. Tomorrow I'll show you around Binnalong and we'll contact a couple of agents to book in house inspections. But until then, you have a good sleep.'

They hugged on the small veranda of the cottage before Helen opened the door.

'Thanks, Lucy—for everything.'

37

———

Two days later, Helen and Lucy set off for Toowoomba in Lucy's car. The four-hour journey was farther than their drive in the Wester Ross area of Scotland, but with the long, straight roads and plenty to talk about, the time passed quickly.

Vonnie opened the door and greeted Lucy with a warm hug. On the way to her house, Lucy had explained how their paths had crossed, and Helen had been fascinated by the story. As Ingrid's mother, Vonnie had accompanied her daughter to Binnalong to meet Lucy after Ingrid's chance encounter with Fergus on the Isle of Skye. That meeting had uncovered an astonishing link between Fergus and his long-lost fiancée from thirty-four years earlier. Determined to trace the mysterious woman, Ingrid had searched against all odds—until a remarkable coincidence had led her to Mandy, Lucy's sister, while working at the Toowoomba hospital. Mandy's distinctive surname had sparked the connection, and from there, the pieces had fallen into place. The rest, as they say, was history.

'Lovely to meet you, Helen. Ingrid's told me how nice it was to spend time together with you and your daughter,' Vonnie said. 'Come in. I have lunch on the table.'

An hour passed quickly as they ate and talked.

After clearing the table, Vonnie dismissed Helen's offer of washing up. 'No. You two had better make the most of the afternoon. I hope you have success with your househunting.' She waved a hand toward the window. 'At least you've got a nice day for it. I'll see you tonight.'

Helen smiled at the petite woman. Smartly dressed, her grey hair neatly coiffured, she oozed the same friendliness of her daughter, despite their vastly different dress codes. Helen had only seen Ingrid wearing jeans, her hair scraped into a ponytail. But with the same welcoming enthusiasm and cheerful disposition, there was no denying they were mother and daughter. She'd felt at ease with both women within minutes of their meeting.

Half an hour later, they were on the road to Crow's Nest before stopping to view two houses north of Highfields that Helen had marked as possibilities. Disappointment swept through her, leaving her hollow. While they might have been appealing, both were larger than she needed and consequently, above her budget.

'Never mind,' Lucy said as they climbed back into the car. 'This is just the beginning. Until you've seen a few, you won't have an idea of the market—but once you do, you'll know "your house" when we see it.'

Helen raised an eyebrow at Lucy's enthusiasm, her own confidence waning.

They checked out another three properties, and after dismissing each one for financial reasons, Helen's stomach sank. Real estate prices really had soared and were continuing to, leaving her meagre budget insufficient for even the most modest of the places they'd viewed.

Lucy reached over and squeezed Helen's hand as they drove back to Toowoomba. 'Don't give up. We'll go south tomorrow and I'm sure you'll see more affordable houses. The Toowoomba area is growing so fast they're bound to be more expensive. We'll find you something—somewhere!'

The following day, after consuming a delicious breakfast of scrambled eggs, bacon, mushrooms, and tomatoes, they waved Vonnie goodbye and drove south.

Properties for sale in the Southern Downs were few and far between. It seemed the current "hot" market ensured many houses were sold before being listed—a "who you know not what you know" situation and another blow to Helen's hopes.

They drove around the Warwick area, visiting a home that bore little resemblance to the description listed, then drove past another two that, abiding by Helen's preferences, didn't warrant an inspection. One was on a busy highway and the other low-lying and at risk of being flooded whenever the Condamine River rose.

With growing despondency, Helen barely spoke as Lucy taxied them farther south to the Stanthorpe district. As they approached Thulimbah, Helen focused on the apple orchards, admiring their orderliness in an effort to cover her dejection. Homes were mostly modest—typical of those built in the post-World-War-Two population boom, but occasionally, a new house or an historic cottage caught her eye.

After pulling into an apple farm, they meandered over to the renovated shed, delighted to find a combination of a wide variety of apple juices, ciders, and byproducts lining the walls of the café. A generous helping of home-made apple pie served with apple cider ice-cream and a pot of tea satisfied both women's hunger and cheered Helen before they once again returned to the car and sat in momentary silence.

'I'm beginning to wonder if I've chosen the wrong area to start over again,' Helen said.

'Don't give up yet. You've selected this district for a

reason. It's not too far from Lisa. The cooler summers and cosy winters will provide the changes you're looking for—and it's a great area for growing flowers and vegetables. Isn't that what you want?'

Helen heaved a sigh. 'I'm not really sure what I want any more. These past couple of months have been ... so different. So much has happened and sometimes I have to pinch myself to ensure its me.'

'I understand. It's because you're free now. No more controlling, abusive husband to upset you. No more farm responsibilities. And no more debt. You're permitted to make any decision you want to from now on—within budget,' she finished with a firm tone, surprising Helen.

Helen sat taller in the seat and straightened her shoulders. 'Okay. Let's go and see what this last agent has got. If they're the same properties we've already visited, then we might as well go home and I'll rethink everything.'

Lucy faced Helen. 'You've had heaps on your mind and you don't have to hurry. Even after I've returned to Skye—which won't be for a while—you know you can continue to stay in my cottage on Binnalong. Meg and Adam would be more than happy to have you around and at least you'll be closer to Lisa than you were on Elizabeth Downs.'

'You're right. I've got a lot to be thankful for. Thank you for being so kind. If I can't find a house to buy, perhaps I could rent somewhere here until the right place comes up.' She looked around her.

Bold, granite hills surrounded the town, the trees naked of their winter clothing—reminding her of her desire to live with four distinct seasons—while fields of orchards and farmland speckled the approaches to the town. It wasn't only the appearance of the area though —it was the feel of it. A creative, positive vibe filled the air while a sense of peace cloaked her every time she stepped out of the vehicle, even if it was to inspect a house she knew would never be hers.

'Good idea. Now, let's make this final call before we check into the motel for the night.'

A bell tingled as they entered the old-fashioned shopfront. On the wooden counter that appeared more like a relic of the turn of the century than a professional office reception bench, an enormous vase of native flowers greeted them. Almost completely hidden behind it as though wanting to remain invisible, an older woman with glasses perched on the end of her nose sat typing furiously on an equally middle-aged computer. She pushed herself to her feet and stepped closer. 'What can I get you?'

Helen stifled a giggle. The woman's question would have been appropriate in a butcher's shop or a café. But here in a real estate agent's time warp, it was received with humour and disbelief. 'I was wondering if you had any listed properties that might be suitable for me?' Helen said.

The little lady waved a hand toward a board in the corner. 'There are a few. Is it a house, a farm, or a business premise you're looking for?'

'A house. Something inexpensive but with a large garden if possible.' Helen named her budget, her heart sinking at the look that crossed the woman's face.

'Oh dear. I doubt you'll find anything for that amount. Southerners coming to Queensland after selling up in places like Melbourne and Sydney have been paying whatever the asking price is here—so sellers are making the most of the situation. Mind you, they have to then buy on the same market so there's plenty out there who're regretting their move.'

'So you have absolutely nothing for us to look at?'

The woman scanned them both up and down, pushing her glasses closer to her eyes as a giant of a man emerged from somewhere out the back.

'How can we help you?' His soft, gentle voice surprised her, and Helen had to stop herself from taking a step forward to hear him better.

She repeated her request, her stomach sinking further as the man shook his head slowly. 'Hmm. That's a tough one.'

'Never mind.' Suddenly she had seen enough and heard the same story once too often. She wanted to get out—run away and rethink her plans. 'I'll keep looking.'

Lucy followed her cue and walked to the door.

'There is one place,' the man said, his face creasing into a frown. 'Not the sort of property I would expect a lady to show interest in—but you can take a look if you wish?'

Helen blanched, holding the door partly open. She wasn't sure if she was honoured to be called a lady—or if she should be affronted at the man's consideration that the property might be unsuitable for a woman.

She dropped the handle, letting the door close with a gentle bang.

'If you would like to follow me, I'll get my car keys and we could take a look?' he said. 'It's not far out of town.'

Helen met Lucy's gaze, recognising Lucy's brief raising of her shoulders as a "Why not?".

Minutes later, they turned off a side road and onto a narrow lane leading to a solitary cottage of indeterminate age. Helen studied the iconic style of yesteryear with the door set in the middle of windows either side and the bull-nosed iron roof over the front veranda.

The women climbed out of Lucy's car slowly, glancing at each other with raised eyebrows.

Lucy whispered, 'Is this what's called a handyman's challenge?'

Helen smiled as somewhere deep within her a frisson of hope blossomed.

38

After stepping cautiously as they walked over the sheep-manure-covered grass inside the front gate, they paused to study the dwelling.

'Circa 1900 or thereabouts, I believe,' the agent said, extending his hand toward Helen. 'Apologies. Name's Gary Broadford.'

The women shook hands with him, formally introducing themselves before Helen turned to consider the cottage.

Broadford—the same as the town on Skye? Perhaps that's a good omen?

Ignoring Gary, she ran her hand along the railing and took a long look at the steps. Although imprinted with manure-tainted sheep hoofprints, they appeared perfectly secure so she walked slowly up and stood on the veranda.

'It seems quite safe?' she said, casting her eyes over the external woodwork.

'Oh yes. Perfectly. The last tenant was a handyman. Did a lot of work on the place in exchange for free rent.'

'And is that pigs I can smell?' Lucy asked, her nose crinkling.

'It was.' Gary laughed—a soft giggle more fitting for a teenage girl rather than a man build like the Hulk. 'The fellow who owned this used to work for the farm next door. He died about a year ago and while the legal stuff took time to sort through, it was rented out through the public trustee—minimal rent in exchange for repairs to make the place saleable. While living here, the tenant reared pigs and grazed sheep in the yard so he didn't have to mow—and apparently no one objected.'

'That explains it. Can we go inside?' Helen asked.

Gary unlocked the door and flung it wide, allowing the scents of freshly hewn timber and new paint to greet them and override the smell of manure.

Slipping off her shoes, Helen padded inside on socked feet, surprised at the contrast from the outside. Although compact, the cottage appeared clean and solidly built. The four main rooms had been painted white and the floors sanded and polished. The basic kitchen contained a bench with a sink and cupboards beneath it while an old wood stove stood nearby. There was a veranda along the back of the cottage with a tiny bathroom at one end and a storeroom at the other.

'Hmm.' Lucy grinned, nudging Helen with her elbow. 'It's minimal but bigger than my cabin. You have two bedrooms and a lounge—and you could fit a fridge and small table in the kitchen. Not sure about much else but perhaps one of those old-fashioned dressers would go against that wall.'

Helen nodded, absorbing Lucy's suggestions while considering the outside. 'How big is the land?' she asked Gary.

'An acre. It was originally the manager's cottage for the farm that surrounds it. At some point the deed was surveyed off and I believe it was gifted to someone—presumably the manager who the owners considered worthy of a retirement package.'

'I like it,' Helen said.

She had never lived in a modern home and had no aspirations to. The cottage radiated a homely welcome despite the cold breeze that blew through the open doors and, to her, that was more important. She bent over the wood stove and inspected it. A small but clean oven, a firebox large enough to burn all night if it was stoked well, and with a polished top that would comfortably hold a heavy bottomed pot and simmering kettle. It would serve for both cooking and heating the house. A smile of excited anticipation crept over her face.

Stepping onto the back veranda, she pinched her nose. The yard was large, smelly, and although dry, was so churned up it could easily be mistaken for a ploughed paddock—minus the straight rows. Nothing resembling vegetation was left. In the back corner next to a new, tightly strained dog-wire fence, a large weeping willow hung over a narrow stream, its contents currently a mere trickle.

A clean slate—perfect to grow vegetables and flowers!

While her mind raced with ideas, she vaguely heard Lucy ask the purchase price. When Gary answered, her head jerked around, her eyes wide.

'Seriously?' She tried to quell her delight.

Not only was the price within her budget, but it was also less than she'd expected to pay, leaving money in the bank to make the changes she wanted.

With the house clean and liveable and the outside smell no worse than other odours she had experienced throughout her life, Helen was puzzled. 'Why did you suggest this place might not be suitable for a woman?'

'Well, you can see for yourself. It's out of town. The outside is nothing more than a smelly farmyard, and there is another thing ...' He paused, his eyes switching from Lucy to Helen and back again.

'Which is?' Helen asked impatiently.

'The owner—that's the one before the tenant moved in—died here.'

'In the house?' Lucy asked.

He shook his head. 'Oh no. A neighbour was moving sheep and saw him lying in the yard. Nothing suspicious. A heart attack.'

'Well,' Helen said in a practical, no-nonsense tone. 'We've all got to die of something and from what you've told us, he was not a young man. Perhaps his time had come—and quite possibly he was pleased he was in his own home right up until it happened.'

'I suppose so. Nevertheless, it is one of those things that women might not like.' His voice held an element of doubt as his eyes met Helen's.

'Well, it won't bother me,' she said.

Bracing herself, Helen made an offer and Gary took a step back with a startled look on his face. It was below the asking price, but after his revelation she'd considered it worth a try.

'I shall have to consult the owner. Perhaps you would care to return to my office so we can contact him and formalise your offer if he accepts?'

'That sounds wonderful. Thank you.' Helen shot Lucy a smile and followed her out of the house.

Nothing was said until they were in the car and driving away.

Then Helen burst out laughing. 'I can't believe it. I've made an offer to buy my very own house!'

'It's wonderful,' Lucy said.

Helen looked at her. She hadn't sounded as enthusiastic as she'd expected. 'What are you thinking?'

'You've got an awful lot of work ahead of you. If your offer's accepted, there might be money left over to employ help. But that's not easy these days ...' She trailed off, her gaze fixed on the road into town.

'Yes, I will be busy. But that's a good thing. I can already picture that backyard, with all the manure and well-ploughed soil courtesy of the pigs making a fabulous garden base. The front yard too. There's not much grass left. Just enough for a small lawn to enhance the garden, and what a wonderful place to grow flowers. And all that manure on the steps will scrub off—or be washed off if we get decent rain.'

Her excitement must have been contagious because within seconds Lucy was offering plant suggestions suitable for a cold, frosty area and rattling off names of flower growers in the district.

'How do you know all that stuff?' Helen asked, astounded. While she had enjoyed helping Lucy plant her Skye garden, she hadn't realised how much interest her friend had in other aspects of flower growing.

'When you first mentioned how much you'd love to grow flowers—and that you were keen to explore the cooler parts of Queensland—I did some research. Did you know there are at least three or four flower and plant growers in this area? A lavender farm, a wholesale supplier who specializes in hydrangeas, and another one whose name I forget—but they grow seasonal flowers using organic and regenerative princi-ples. You might be able to work with them?'

'Oh Lucy, you really are the best friend ever.'

Lucy shot her a grin as they pulled up outside the agent's office. 'One step at a time, my friend. Let's get this negotiation sorted and papers signed first, then we'll head to the motel via the cafe. I reckon a nice coffee is in order. Agree?'

Helen tipped her head back and laughed. 'I do.'

39

———

Michael parked outside the hospital, remaining motionless as he stared at the building. Brick with a historical exterior that radiated grace yet maintained an austere facade. Its size was welcoming, being so much smaller than the sprawling high-rise constructions of large cities. And the gardens, although frost-affected, appeared tidy and well kept. He imagined them in spring. Perhaps they would be full of tulips and daffodils. He'd never been a gardener, but his short sojourn to Scotland had opened his eyes to the beauty and vibrance that plants and flowers could bring. But now he was here—a twenty-bed hospital in a small Queensland country town offering all the basic care required despite being a far cry from the massive Sydney hospital.

He got out of the car, gasping as the icy wind stole

his breath. Zipping his jacket, he walked up the steps to the double-width front doors.

Minutes later, he found himself in a cosy room with high ceilings having his hand gripped tightly by a woman of indeterminate age.

Tall and solidly built, her hair was scraped into a bun, her face a mix of apprehension and relief. 'We're pleased to welcome you to our town and our much-valued hospital, Doctor Blakeney. I'm Paula Stewart, director of nursing. We spoke on the phone.'

'Ahh, yes. Thank you for inviting me. I'm looking forward to working with you and your staff.'

The creases around her mouth disappeared as the loose skin stretched into a wide smile, altering her appearance from dour to delightful. 'As you would know, getting doctors out of the cities and into regional areas is tricky so we're very pleased to have you join us.' She picked up a pair of glasses and placed them on her nose before switching to a more businesslike tone.

'I thought I would show you around today, introduce you to some of the team, and then you'd have the weekend to settle into your accommodation before you begin official duties on Monday.'

'Sounds wonderful. Thank you.'

Despite the winter chill outside, within the thick walls of the hospital, it was warm—so much so that Michael not only unzipped his jacket but removed it altogether.

An hour passed as the two of them strolled from emergency to wards, treatment rooms to palliative care. In all areas, there was a softness to the atmosphere that surprised Michael. He couldn't put his finger on it but absorbed it all the same. Perhaps it was the more relaxed pace of life. Or perhaps it was the friendliness of those he met. Whatever it was, Michael's hopes soared.

This is more like it.

'We've booked you a motel room for tonight while your quarters are being cleaned,' Paula said. 'I hope you like your unit. It's not huge and has been vacant for a while. Our previous doctor was married with a family so owned his own home here in town. But, prior to that, we had a young doctor who'd been through a traumatic divorce, and he was very happy there.

'I'm sure it will be perfect. Thank you, Paula.'

'When you're ready, just pop into reception in the morning and someone will give you the keys.'

Michael waited. 'Umm. Where are these quarters?'

She planted the heel of her hand on her forehead and groaned. 'Good grief. I'm so sorry. I should have taken you there first.' Beckoning him to follow, she turned and headed for a side door.

He trailed her across the grassy area toward a second brick building set fifty metres from the hospital grounds.

'Decades ago, this was the staff quarters,' Paula

said. 'It sat empty for a while, then when it became obvious that attracting doctors to these rural areas was nigh on impossible, we—that is the community —got together and fundraised. With generous donations from local businesses and families, we also applied for a government grant and were able to have the building restored and converted into two nice apartments. One is used for those who live too far away to travel back and forth and need to be close to a loved one. Of course, there is a small charge for this and it is most often used by the family of a palliative patient. The other—your new home—is the one facing away from town. It offers lovely views to the hills.'

Inside the apartment, a woman cleaning the windows turned to say hello.

Michael's gaze roved around, taking in the cosy lounge area with its leather couch and wide-screen television. A well-arranged kitchen with a square table and two chairs in one corner opened onto a small balcony. Off the lounge, a generous bedroom led to a bathroom—functional and nicely decorated in warm earthy tones.

'Those carports over there are for your vehicle and the car belonging to any family staying next door. I'm sure you won't be bothered by noise. There are strict rules here and if anyone staying in the other unit disobeys them, there are consequences.' Paula frowned as she spoke. 'Not that we've ever had any problems—just saying.'

Their smiles met briefly before they turned to leave.

TAKING HIS TIME, Michael drove slowly around the town before seeking the motel Paula had directed him to. He removed only his overnight bag from the car and checked in. Then, with his jacket fastened and a scarf wound around his neck, he set off for a walk along Quart Pot Creek.

Pleasantly relaxed in the chilly air, he strode out, marching briskly to warm up initially then slowing to better absorb his surroundings. His stomach rumbled. He thought back to his previous meal and glanced at his watch. It had been a toasted sandwich and a cup of coffee five hours earlier. No wonder his insides were protesting.

Seeking a suitable venue for dinner as the wintry sun set, he increased his stride again and made for the main street, the evening chill wrapping around him. Ahead, two women walked arm in arm toward him, too busy talking to notice him until only metres away.

His heart leapt. With wide, disbelieving eyes, his smile widened. It couldn't be, could it?

It was—two of the nicest people he could wish to meet. Helen and Lucy.

In an instant, their eyes met.

Helen recognised him seconds before Lucy and hauled her friend to a halt. 'Michael?' she said. 'It is! Michael!'

They greeted each other with hugs and jubilant grins.

'What brings you here?' Helen asked.

'Work. You're looking at the newly appointed hospital doctor.'

Helen's hand flew to her mouth, her smile widening. 'That's amazing.'

'And what exciting event has attracted you ladies to Stanthorpe?' Michael asked.

'Househunting. I-I've just made an offer on a cottage!' Her voice rose in a disbelieving squeak.

'Really? I thought you were thinking of somewhere closer to Lisa—or Toowoomba?'

'I was.'

Lucy interrupted then. 'Dinner? We were on our way to "Anna's" restaurant. We've made a booking but I'm sure they'd fit you in if you'd like to join us. We can continue talking there.'

'Sounds wonderful,' he said. 'Apparently we've both got something to celebrate.'

As they walked side by side, the comfortable,

happy glow that affected him when he'd been with Helen previously, returned.

He'd planned to wait a few days at the hospital before telling anyone, wanting to be certain his decision was the right one. Even Julian was still unaware his father would be living and working only a couple of hours away—and now, with Helen by his side, he was glad it was a surprise for them both.

Finding her again, so soon after their time on Skye and in this same small town far from her own world, seemed too perfect to be chance. Some things were just meant to be.

40

___

Their meal was both delicious and filled with joy. Michael listened intently, a soft smile on his face as Helen shared the description of the cottage.

'And the pig poo?' Michael chuckled. 'How are you going to live with that?' He wrinkled his nose.

'You might be horrified,' Helen said. 'But we're used to all types of smells on a farm, and I know that once I've got hold of a rotary hoe and run it over the area, most of it will be well churned into the dirt and perfect for planting into. I'll probably leave it fallow for a while—give myself time to get the cottage sorted out and find a job somewhere.' She grimaced. 'I may have been able to purchase a house, but there won't be much left in the bank and I've got to eat.'

The admiration in Michael's eyes was plain to see. 'I've got to hand it to you. You're one tough lady.'

'Yeah, well. I've had to be. Now—tell us about yourself. What made you move to Queensland?'

For a few seconds, no one said anything.

The women stared at Michael, and he looked straight into Helen's eyes. 'You.'

Her stomach flipped as though lifted by a hundred butterflies. 'Me?'

'Yes. Throughout our time together on Skye, you never once complained—even though I knew you would have been in pain at times after your accident. I admire you—all you have been through, even to the point of coping with being a suspect in your husband's death. Most women would have fallen in a heap—wouldn't they?'

Lucy and Helen simultaneously shook their heads.

'You don't know us very well, do you?' Lucy laughed. 'We're tougher than you think.'

'I realise that now. Perhaps it's because the majority of women I've met have been patients—and there's usually a good reason for them to complain.' He grinned. 'Anyway, I think some of your strength rubbed off on me—encouraged me to make changes in my life.'

They laughed as the wait staff arrived at their table with the dessert menu.

An hour later, satiated by the delicious Italian food,

they wandered out of the restaurant and into the frosty night. Overhead, the moonlight glimmered on the thin layer of ice coating the grassy berm, setting it alight with a silvery sparkle.

'This is what I really want to live with,' Helen said, stepping onto the ice and smiling as it crunched beneath her feet. 'Four seasons. I've heard it even snows here sometimes. How good is that?' Her voice was high with childish delight.

'Wait until you've experienced a Scottish winter,' Lucy said drily. 'The snow isn't quite the novelty it is here.'

The conversation flowed again from Scottish winters to hot Queensland summers and everything in between as they ambled along the footpath toward Lucy and Helen's motel.

'What time are you ladies heading off in the morning?' Michael asked.

'When we're ready, I guess. I'm relieved the owner accepted my offer and we don't need to rush anywhere today. I half-expected him to want more but it's good to know I'll have something to live on while I set up the house and garden and investigate employment opportunities.'

They reached the motel and stood outside for a minute, stamping their feet to keep warm.

'What about we have breakfast together?' Michael said. 'My motel's only a little farther up the road. I'll walk down to meet you and we could go to a café in the main street. Then, when you ladies are ready to leave, I'll check out of my motel and move into the salubrious chez staff quarters.'

Helen smiled while Lucy nodded.

'Sounds like a fabulous idea,' Helen said.

He leaned forward and kissed each of them on the cheek, holding Helen's hand for a few seconds longer than he did Lucy's. 'Better let you get inside before you freeze. See you in the morning.'

Helen's wide grin remained as she gave him a small wave before following Lucy into their room.

Flopping on to the bed, she raised her arms and folded them behind her head. 'What an amazing day. I was getting a bit worried I'd never find the right place for me. But now ...'

'Pfft. I think we were very lucky we popped into that last agent's office,' Lucy said.

They laughed and a vision of the enormous Gary and his tiny assistant entered Helen's head. 'And to think he was reluctant to show us the cottage because "It's not the sort of property I would expect a lady to show interest in".'

'I know! And now ... Michael. This is definitely the right place for you—and probably the best decision you've made for years.' Lucy reached out and hugged Helen. 'Congratulations. Your new life has begun.'

HELEN PACKED her bag the following morning, reluctant to leave her soon-to-be new town. Despite there being at least two weeks before she could move in—and that would only be if the public trustee and family agreed on a quick contract—the town seemed to wrap its arms around her like a warm cloak.

Her insides fluttered with anticipation. Michael was here! Like her, this town was to be his new home. Incredulity swept through her once again. Suppressing all thoughts of the years past and life on Elizabeth Downs, she brushed her hair, applied lipstick, and picked up her handbag, her mind racing.

It would be only a temporary goodbye. After breakfast, she and Lucy would return to Binnalong where she would stay while the necessary paperwork was processed, arrangements were made for her belongings to be trucked south from Shelley and Bill's property—a feat that would no doubt require Tim's expertise and trucking connections—and a shopping list was considered for the purchase of new furniture items she would need to begin life in such a small home. The heavy, leather lounge suite, wide double-door fridge, and chunky eight-seater dining table would have to be sold or donated to charity. She would not be sorry about that.

'Ready?' Lucy asked, breaking Helen's thoughts.

'Aren't we waiting for Michael?'

'Yes—and here he is.'

Helen opened the door, beaming as Michael crossed the motel car park.

'Morning, ladies. Hungry?'

'I'm starving,' Lucy said.

Helen and Michael laughed. 'So nothing's changed then,' Michael said.

'Nope. I'm always hungry when I travel,' Lucy said. 'I think it's visiting these lovely little towns with cafés in the main street that allow their delicious aromas of coffee and fresh-baked goodies to drift out the doors. It makes me want to dive into each one and sample the produce.'

Once again, the happy trio strode along the road, crossed the bridge onto the high street, and turned into the first café they came to, despite it being filled with customers.

'Good sign?' Michael said as he pushed the door open and waved the women through ahead of him.

While Lucy hurried to claim the only available table, Helen and Michael joined the queue at the counter and studied the menu.

'My shout,' Michael said. 'You order what you'd like then swap places with Lucy while I order mine.'

Aware of the difference in their budgets, Helen understood it was his subtle way of preventing any embarrassment on her part, but there were times when she wished she could reciprocate and not have to consider whether or not she could afford dessert or a second cup of coffee. She dearly hoped that one day she would—but for now was grateful for Michael's generosity.

Jack's behaviour toward her had been the opposite and even now, hundreds of kilometres from his grave, a shiver ran up her spine as she was reminded of his glowering expression on the rare occasions she'd suggested they have a meal out. After the children left home, she had tried to improve their relationship—to search for a little romance in their lives. She'd suggested they dine out once in a while or invite Shelley and Bill for dinner. But he'd always snorted derisively and made some pathetic excuse—he needed to get up earlier than usual the following morning because so-and-so was delivering seed or coming to pick up a load of hay, or he'd helped Bill all day and was tired of talking. But for some reason it was alright for him to head into town for a drink—or several—at the local pub, particularly if there was a pretty woman close by. Some things never changed.

After thanking Michael again for his kindness an hour later, he strode away—this time leaving the memory of his kiss lingering on her lips, fire in her soul, and hope in her heart.

41

———

'That's fabulous news, Mum,' Lisa's shrieked with delight. 'How amazing is it that you and Michael will be living in the same town—and neither of you knew the other would be there? When Julian has a couple of days off, we'll be able to come over and visit you both.'

'Sounds great.' Her daughter's enthusiasm warmed Helen's heart. 'I'll miss seeing the boys as often, living so far away, but Tim and Heidi are flat out with the business. You never know, Tim might have to truck stock down this way. And Steve—well, who knows where or when either of us will see him. Once the wet season gets underway and his workload eases, he might decide to fly down for a visit too.'

'He will—and thank goodness for video calls and mobile phones in the meantime.'

They chatted about Lisa's work, the outings and events she and Julian had shared over the previous couple of weeks, and then the conversation turned to Jack's death.

'Have you heard any more?' Lisa asked.

'A brief update but nothing solid. I don't think they believe Warren had anything to do with your dad's accident, but it seems there's something else they're investigating—and are not willing to share that information yet.'

'Hopefully no news is good news?' Lisa said.

Helen sighed. 'Yes.'

Her children had seen enough. Experienced enough. But they were adults and there was nothing more she could do to protect them. The truth would be revealed in time—and she just hoped the news would be positive.

As though fated, minutes after her call with Lisa, Helen's phone rang again.

Private number.

Her chest tightened, her pulse pounding as she swiped the green icon. 'Hello?'

'Hello, Helen. Russell Seal here. Thought you'd like an update.'

She blinked rapidly. No longer concerned about

herself—they'd already confirmed she was not a suspect—what else had they found?

'Oh. Yes. Thank you.'

The detective cleared his throat. 'We've had an interesting couple of days with your ex-employee—Warren Peck.'

Her stomach sank. She sucked in a breath and held it, waiting for deliverance.

'He's been generous with his information—no doubt to convince us he had nothing to do with either your husband's death or the illegal dealings Jack was involved in. And as we haven't found anything to sway blame his way, we are bound by the evidence that has been revealed.'

'Which is?' *Get to the point!*

'Your husband was involved in a chop-chop syndicate.'

'A what?' Helen's eyes goggled.

'Chop-chop—illegal tobacco, cigarettes, and vapes.'

'But ... why?' The moment the words were out of her mouth, she clamped her lips tightly, her mind racing. She'd heard the term "chop-chop" used before but had never given it much thought.

Russell emitted a weird grunting noise, sounding like he may have been choking back a laugh.

'Money. All he had to do was provide storage for large amounts of contraband in return for substantial advance payments. The problem was he didn't keep his side of the bargain. Instead of building the shed he'd agreed to, he invested the money in your farm—new tractor, fencing, and cattle yards apparently. Mr Peck declares he knew nothing about where the money was coming from, but when Jack let it slip after having too much to drink one evening, they had words and Jack said he'd received an advance payment. According to Mr Peck, Warren told Jack he wanted nothing to do with the deal and was leaving. But when Jack threatened to tell police it had been Warren's idea if he did, Warren agreed to remain until the sorghum was harvested.'

Helen almost fell off the chair. Jack may have had mood problems and not treated his family as kindly as they deserved, but nothing made sense. She knew him well enough to feel sure the illegal dealings were not the way he operated. Someone else had to have organised it and set him up as a perfect candidate.

'So who is behind this ... crime?'

'That's what we're working on now. We've been following up on a few leads coming out of Asia. It may not prove whether Jack's death was accidental or deliberate—at this stage there has been no evidence to confirm that—but it does explain your husband's actions prior to his death, including storing materials for a shed that Mr Peck understood was supposed to have been erected somewhere inconspicuous on your property.'

Helen slumped further in the chair, grateful she was sitting down. How long had this been going on? She cast her mind back to the last drought. 2017 to 2019 had been their worst years. It had coincided with Jack's aggression and moodiness increasing. At the time, she'd been worried about him. Had it been depression? But then the rain came, and Jack's moods had improved—slightly.

A few years later, he'd become more evasive, particularly with the farm books—and it occurred to her that this change had coincided with Warren's arrival. Again, her insides knotted with anger and remorse. She had missed something. If only she'd taken the time to watch him more instead of bowing her head and working harder in an effort to prove how important she was to both him and the success of their farm.

'So ...' Detective Seal's gravelly voice penetrated her thoughts. 'I'll let you know more when our enquiries are complete.'

'Thank you.'

Detective Seal said goodbye and hung up.

She wanted to curl in a ball—the shock of hearing her husband had been involved in illegal tobacco smuggling too much to bear. Right under her nose! Was she at fault? She sat bolt upright. Something about Warren Peck's story niggled—didn't ring true.

Glancing down at her phone, she groaned. She didn't have Russell Seal's number to ring him back.

She slumped against the wall, head throbbing. The worry that the sale might fall apart, stopping her from securing the cottage or starting her new life, weighed heavily on her.

Thoughts swirled as she replayed events and possibilities. If a crime hung over the history of Elizabeth Downs, would that mean the contract would be delayed—or worse still, cancelled? Who, other than a lawyer, might know what happened with property contracts in these cases? Clint! Behind his kind, discreet manner, she was certain he would have dealt with unusual real estate situations.

She prodded her phone and waited.

'Hello, Helen. How are you?'

'Sorry to bother you ... I-I was wondering if you knew about the findings surrounding Jack's death and how that affects the contract on Elizabeth Downs?'

His slow intake of breath sounded before he spoke. 'I've had a discussion with Detective Seal—so yes, I am aware there has been a problem. However, none of that interferes with the sale or settlement. The police inspected the shed kit before Bill and Shelley collected it. It was the only piece of evidence on Elizabeth Downs relating to Jack's activities and there's no information of payment or delivery. The situation would have been far more complicated if Jack were still alive, but for the moment anyway, establishing who's behind this organisation is their primary goal. My understanding is that Jack's death is just a stepping stone in the search for something much bigger.'

Her shoulders sagged. 'Thank goodness.'

'How are you getting on with your search for a new home?'

Helen gave Clint a description of the cottage, and they both laughed when she described the pig-ploughed back yard.

'Yes. I'm sure that would have put off a few potential buyers. But not you, Helen. You're the strongest woman I've ever met.'

His words shocked Helen into momentary silence as she remembered Michael's similar comment. 'Really? I'm not feeling it.'

'Don't think like that,' he said gently. 'Remember Steve and I've been mates since we were little kids. He never said much but I didn't have to be Einstein to read between the lines. It was you who kept that family from going under. You who kept your children safe and who turned a smiling face to everyone you met, regardless of gossip.'

Helen straightened as he spoke—the wise young friend of her son. His confidence drew strength from somewhere deep inside her, as though encasing her body and soul in an invisible coat of armour.

'Thank you, Clint.' She pressed a hand against her chest, willing her mind to live up to Clint's praise.

'I mean it, Helen. Don't worry about things at this

end of the deal. Between the bank and police, every-thing will sort itself out. The buyers' balance will be transferred into your account on settlement day. It won't be long and you'll never have to worry about Elizabeth Downs again.'

But despite Clint's confidence, Helen's gut heaved with fear and confusion. If Jack had used the advance Warren mentioned, courtesy of a criminal syndicate to improve Elizabeth Downs, how come there was so much debt? Wouldn't the money have resolved their financial worries and they wouldn't have owed money to anyone? Or had Jack never actually received the advance the detective spoke of and borrowed instead to make the changes on the farm, believing that when the deal was up and running, he would pay back the debt and no one, especially Helen, would ever know?

That was it! She had to contact Detective Seal. Jack had his faults—she knew that better than most. But he'd loved Elizabeth Downs and he'd loved farming. If he'd never actually received any money prior to his death, what was he guilty of other than forging her name in order to obtain enough funds to provide the farm with the tools and improvements needed to gain a bigger return?

Fierce determination flourished inside her as the puzzle unravelled in her head. Perhaps there was a syndicate dealing in illegal chop-chop. Perhaps Jack had been approached and tempted to participate. But someone had to have put Jack's name forward. Someone had to have talked him into it and there was only one person she could think of, regardless of what Detective Seal believed.

Warren Peck.

42

'Helen!'

Helen jumped to her feet, her thoughts scattering as Lucy's voice rang out across the yard to the cabin porch at Binnalong.

Lucy jogged toward her and leaned a hand on the veranda post, a worried frown on her face. 'Meg's in labour. I'm going with them to the hospital now. Would you mind feeding the chooks and letting the dogs off for a run?'

'Of course not. You go. Let me know if there's anything else you need me to do.'

'Thanks. They probably don't need me, but you know what it's like when you live out of town. I don't want Adam driving if the baby comes faster than expected or Meg gets distressed.'

'Go, Lucy. Leave everything else to me.' Helen

dismissed her friend with a confident smile. She would be fine.

The morning dragged as she waited for news. Helen completed the chores, wandered around the garden, prepared a crockpot dinner for the evening, and made herself a cup of tea. Then, glancing at her watch for the umpteenth time, she rang Michael.

'Hello.' There was a smile in his voice as he answered.

'Hi there. How's moving going?'

'It's done,' he laughed. 'Two suitcases, my sound system, and a couple of boxes of books and personal stuff doesn't take long. I'm now sitting in the sun enjoying a cup of tea.'

'Snap. I'm doing the same.'

'What's happening at Binnalong?'

Helen shared the news of the impending birth and their trouble-free drive back to the property the previous day.

Then she took a deep breath. 'Can I run something by you?'

'Sure. Fire away.'

'As you know, the police have been investigating Jack's death due to something they know about but haven't yet solved. I received a call from the detective with an update that doesn't make sense to me, and I have this gut feeling that they're "barking up the wrong tree" as the saying goes. Before I ring the police to share my thoughts, I wondered if you would give me your opinion please?'

'Of course, Helen. I know nothing about solving crimes—except what I watch on television and movies of course. But I'm always here to listen. Fire away.'

Beginning with Jack's death, Helen shared every piece of the journey and every applicable snippet of history she could to enable Michael to understand the man who'd died, the situation on the farm, and the disconnect between the debt and the supposed "advance" payment.

When she finished minutes later, there was a moment's silence between them.

'Hmm,' Michael said. 'I agree with you. Where's the evidence that Jack was paid an advance? The truth is more likely to be the opposite. He racked up debts so huge he couldn't afford to repay them from the proceeds of the farm alone. So you're right, if he was expecting an advance payment for something he was talked into doing, he may have borrowed, knowing he could repay it once the advance arrived. But why didn't he build the shed? Clearly it was purchased from somewhere?' His voice faded. 'Unless he didn't buy it. Perhaps it was delivered on the understanding he was to erect it within a certain time period. But by then he was preoccupied with improving the farm, so delayed the construction and ... oh my goodness.' He stopped talking abruptly.

'What is it?' Helen asked.

'His fall could have been a complete accident. What if he was thinking about the whole chop-chop deal thing and genuinely slipped from lack of concentration?'

Horror morphed inside Helen.

'I'm thinking what I suspect you are too. I reckon you need to get back to that detective for a chat,' Michael said.

'Thank you. I guess I've been so angry about everything for so long, I haven't been able to filter through the facts. Now it's pretty clear to me—there are things the police should know but don't. And although our marriage was not a happy one, for Jack's sake and to remove any doubt he was guilty of hoarding contraband, I need to act now.'

'I agree,' Michael said. 'Let me know how you get on.'

'I will.'

'And Helen ...'

'Yes?'

'I'm looking forward to you moving here.'

A smile swept across her face, but she was too anxious to let it dwell. The complications of Jack's accident, the messy situation with their ex-employee, and her stupid, naïve lack of insight blocked everything else from her mind. She had to get in touch with the team immediately.

'Me too,' she said.

THE PHONE RANG for so long she was about to hang up when a breathless voice answered.

'Good morning. Constable Matthews speaking.'

'Helen Gooding here. I'd like to speak with Detective Seal please.'

After being shuffled from one extension to another, she was eventually connected with the correct team for a message to be taken by a junior officer. She reassured Helen that Detective Seal would call her back—and an hour later, her phone lit up with "Private Number".

'I'm sorry to have kept you waiting,' he said. 'We've had to reinterview Warren Peck as evidence has come to hand that the owner of the green Mercedes car seen near your property was in fact looking for Mr Peck.'

'Oh!' The comment threw Helen and for a few seconds, she didn't speak.

'Now, I understand you have information you'd like to share.'

'Yes, I do. I thought about what you told me earlier and ... I apologise if this sounds rude, but what you said didn't make sense. You see, when Jack died, I was made aware that our financial position was nothing like what it should have been.'

'I see.' His voice was sharp, hinting she had better

not be wasting his time. 'Would you mind if we record this conversation?'

'Not at all. Please do.'

She calmly recited the history of the farm debts, Jack's forgery of her signature, and the reason the property had to be sold.

'And you had no idea why he borrowed such a large sum of money?'

'No. I was unaware of the additional loan. We'd always had a mortgage which he regularly assured me was under control. He led me to believe the improvements to the farm, including the new tractor, were all the result of good cattle and grain sales. Jack was particular about bookkeeping and preferred to deal with it himself, so I didn't feel it necessary to check.'

She stopped short, pausing while her seething stomach settled. Shame filled her. The farm had been a partnership—at least so far as the workload went. And while their relationship wasn't what she wanted, she had been confident—even pleased when Jack announced the cattle sale and previous year's crop had turned their finances around. She should have guessed. Asked more questions. Even demanded to know exact costs. But she hadn't dared. He'd kept the computer password protected and out of bounds, which is why she had used her restaurant wages to buy a laptop, set up an email address, and mostly corresponded with Tim, Steve, and Lisa—and her friends,

Lucy and Roslyn—leaving the business side of farming to Jack.

'The amount borrowed was enough to provide improvements for our farm—and although it's possible Warren Peck's story about the chop-chop storage and advance payment could be true, if it is I'd like to believe Jack only accrued those debts because of the promise of an advance—the one Warren mentioned to you. And, given that Warren Peck has avoided me as much as he could throughout his employment, I also believe that there's a good chance the idea—and the links to the organisers of this money-making scheme—would have been Warren's, not Jack's.'

'Hmm. I understand what you're saying, Mrs Gooding.'

She waited while he drew a noisy breath and continued.

'Leave it with me. We'll be looking into this further. I'll call you again with a progress report.'

'Thank you.'

After ending the call, Helen sat on the cabin veranda, blindly staring at the paddocks surrounding her and wishing she could fall asleep and wake to find all this nonsense had been a dream—or an imaginary nightmare.

43

It was almost dark by the time Lucy returned to Binnalong, elated and exhausted.

Helen ran down the steps to meet her as she stopped in front of the homestead. 'Has the baby arrived?'

'Yes. Took his time, but he's here and everyone is healthy and super excited. At least Adam and Meg are anyway.' Lucy looked at Helen and laughed. 'You can stop worrying now.'

Helen straightened her frown with a smile. 'Sorry. I'm not worrying about the baby. I mean, I was thinking of everyone but that's not what's on my mind.'

'Oh? I'm gasping for a cuppa and some dinner. Let's go inside and talk about the day.'

Thankful she had prepared a slow-cooked meal

early in the day, Helen made a pot of tea while Lucy showered and changed her clothes.

'It's so hot in the hospitals, isn't it?' she said. 'I didn't think about it when I dashed off this morning. I was so worried about Meg I didn't change so I sat there in my winter layers and cooked.'

'Have they named the baby?' Helen asked.

'Yes. Connor Robert. They both liked Connor and as you know, Robert was Adam's father's name.' She continued relating the day's events while they drank the tea.

Eventually, she ran out of news and stopped suddenly. 'I'm sorry for babbling on. You mentioned you were worried, but not about the baby. So, tell me, what's been going on?'

For the third time that day, Helen repeated the conversations she'd had with both the detective and Michael.

'So, all this time, the police have known something about this syndicate?' Lucy shook her head. 'They had to have suspected something. That's why they were hinting at Jack's death not being accidental, wasn't it? All because he's not here to tell his side of the story, leaving that sleazy Warren Peck to blame it all on Jack. I hope he goes down for this—Warren, that is,' she finished with an angry huff.

'You're right. But you know as well as I do, unless

there's evidence to support our thoughts, he'll get away with it.'

'Unless ...' Lucy put her index finger to her upper lip. 'That green car, the one that was searching for Warren. If they've established who owns it and find out why he was looking for Warren, the truth might just be revealed.'

Helen chuckled. 'I think we've read too many Miss Marple stories.'

Her mood became serious again. 'But you're right. Now I've had a talk with Detective Seal, I have to trust him to get to the bottom of it—and I do feel much better. There's been something needling me ever since he rang when we were in Scotland. Jack had his faults, but believing he was involved in something like this is not what I want to remember. He did the wrong thing by forging my signature and hiding the financial situation, but I have to believe he did what he did because he thought he was helping the farm—and us both.'

'You're a good person, Helen. I'm sure you're right —but now I'd like to eat some of that delicious curry I can smell.'

They smiled at each other as Lucy took two bowls from the cupboard and removed the lid from the slow cooker.

OVER THE FOLLOWING DAYS, Helen talked with Detective Seal, Lucy video-called Fergus daily, Meg and baby Connor returned home to Binnalong, the contract on Helen's new home was completed, and the funds were transferred to the conveyancing solicitors trust account in readiness for settlement day.

Helen took the opportunity to drive back to Shelley's. Although she was tempted to drive past Elizabeth Downs, instead she headed directly to her friend's house, convincing herself there would be no visible change yet and even if there was, it was no longer her property.

The first twenty-four hours with Bill and Shelley were busy—filled with sorting out what needed to be trucked to Helen's new home and what could be sold or given away.

'Leave it with me,' Shelley said firmly. 'I know of a young refugee couple who've recently arrived and have little more than their clothes. If you don't mind, I'd like to offer the furniture you don't need to them?'

'Perfect,' Helen said. It was a relief—and one thing closer to settling into her the cottage. She was sure she'd be able to pick up essential second-hand bits and pieces and, she might actually treat herself to a brand-new sofa. It would need to be compact but that was fine—it only had to be big enough to seat two people.

A smile flickered across her face. Michael had messaged to say he had enjoyed his first few days in the hospital and was looking forward to her returning to Stanthorpe so they could have a celebratory dinner together—just the two of them.

It was something she was excited about. But before she could truly move on, she waited anxiously for Detective Seal to finalise the investigation into Jack's death and to confirm whether or not he had committed an offense.

After letting Shelley talk her into staying a second night before attempting the long drive south, Helen was feeding the chooks—her chooks who appeared to have settled into their rather upmarket new pen nicely —when Bill tore into the yard in his ute, the window down and his arm crooked on the door sill. He'd left in the dark, his once-a-week job as a stockman at the local saleyards requiring an early start.

'Hey, Helen!' he yelled. 'Got some good news for ya.'

She hurried toward him as Shelley approached from the house.

'Word has it that Warren Peck's been arrested.'

'Really?' The surge of incredulity broke her concentration and she almost stumbled. 'On what charge? And what does that mean for Jack, even though he's no longer here?'

Bill shrugged. 'I reckon you'll know pretty soon. That detective fellow should be updating you any tick of the clock.'

A tingling warmth spread through Helen. There'd always been something about that man. From the first time they'd met, a gut feeling had hinted to her that perhaps he wasn't who he said he was. Regardless, he hadn't been a good influence on Jack—no matter what work ethics he'd displayed publicly. And for that, she had paid the price.

They didn't have to wait long. Shelley was clearing away the breakfast plates when Helen's phone rang.

'That'll be him,' Bill said.

Helen glanced at the screen and grinned. 'Looks like it.'

'Hello?' She punched the speaker icon and placed the phone on the table between them.

'Detective Seal here, Mrs Gooding. It appears your suspicions were well-founded. The owner of the green Mercedes has been located and brought in for questioning. It took some coaxing, but he eventually confirmed he and Peck were both part of an illegal importing syndicate for tobacco and other goods—possibly in the hope he'll get away with a lighter sentence.'

Helen sat back in her chair, her eyebrows raised as she glanced from Bill to Shelley. 'So how did Jack get involved?' she asked.

'Jung Lee admitted he was hired to supervise and coordinate the storage facilities for north Queensland. Further investigations revealed Warren Peck has been involved in similar cases before—under his real name of Wayne Proctor. It was his job to blend into the rural workforce using his experience and knowledge of farming. He preyed on the gullible, and I'm afraid to say your husband proved to be the perfect candidate. It appears he didn't take much convincing to put his hand out for a generous payment—in exchange for building appropriate storage facilities and keeping his mouth shut.'

'Which didn't happen?' Helen asked.

'No. It seems he and Mr Peck had experienced their own wars over the still-to-be-completed shed. But Peck wasn't as smart as he believed he was. He thought Mr Lee had given Jack the promised advance—which was what they were using to improve your property with. So, when Jack died—accidentally—and we investigated, as Jack's employee, Peck was suspect number one. I apologise for putting you through what must have felt like irrelevant questioning. However, we were trying to establish who, other than you, may have seen your husband that day and whether you had any involvement.' He paused for a moment and cleared his throat. 'When you told me about the accrued debts the other day, Peck was questioned again. He appeared genuinely confused, unaware Jack had borrowed money to complete the farm improvements. The tale Mr Peck-slash-Proctor spun about Jack receiving the advance was his ploy to cover his involvement by laying the blame on your husband.'

Helen blew out a long breath as her brain spun with the information. 'So what happens now?'

'For you, nothing. For Jack, also nothing. His involvement in this issue is no longer relevant and while it appears he made some inappropriate decisions, we're unable to prefer charges on a deceased person. The case will continue but you can be reassured neither Jack's nor your names will be mentioned again. You are free to live your life without worry, Mrs Gooding. And once again, I apologise for having to involve you in our investigations.'

All three of them shared astonished, wide-eyed relieved expressions before looking back at the phone on the table. 'Thank you. Goodbye—and good luck.' Helen reached out and cleared her phone in the silence that followed.

Eventually, Bill spoke. 'Who would have thought it, ay? I never did like that Peck. Got his just desserts if you ask me.'

Shelley stood and walked to the kettle, filled it, and switched it on. 'I know situations like this call for something stronger, but as it's not even ten o'clock yet, a cup of tea will have to do.'

44

It was another hour before Helen finished making phone calls to her children, Lucy, and Michael.

'That's amazing,' Michael said, echoing the comments of the others.

'It's more than amazing,' Helen laughed. 'It's liberating! Ever since Jack died this ... thing has hung over my head. I kept seeing him, feeling his presence, and thinking I was going mad—that he was haunting me.'

'You didn't say.' Michael's soft voice filled with compassion.

'Of course not. You might have agreed.'

They both hooted with laughter as a vague dizziness swayed Helen. She felt lighter, as though she'd shed a heavy wool coat. Perhaps it had been real. Perhaps Jack had been hovering over her. Not to threaten or frighten her but to attempt to convey the truth.

Her heart filled with joy, anticipation, and excitement. She was truly free and had a whole new life ahead of her.

'When are you planning to arrive at your new home?' Michael asked.

'I'm going to Lucy's today. Settlement day is Thursday, so I'll leave early that day to drive to Stanthorpe and stay in a motel. I've arranged the furniture and what-not to be delivered on Friday morning so I can supervise its arrival and have all weekend to get organised.'

'That sounds wonderful. I can't wait to see you again—and of course I'll be there to help.'

Her chest swelled, the wonder of feeling so happy blossoming inside her. 'Thank you. See you on Thursday?'

'You bet ... and Helen, I have something I want to tell you.'

'Oh? Good or bad?'

'Good now. But it could have been bad. It was a legal thing—something that cropped up when I was in Scotland. The reason I had to come home early.'

Helen's happiness wavered as she processed this information. "Is it ... something I need to know?'

'Probably not. But I'd like to share it with you so you can understand me better. You've gone through so much in the past few months and I feel privileged that you confided in me. I would like to start off afresh—with no skeletons in the cupboard.'

Secretly chuffed, a contented smile crept across her face. 'Then I look forward to hearing your story.'

DRIVING into Stanthorpe late on Thursday afternoon, a strange feeling crept over Helen—one she had never experienced and one she couldn't describe. Could it be wonder? Wonder if she had made the right decision? Wonder if she was the same person she'd been only months earlier?

That's it. I'm not. My eyes have been opened and I've been offered another chance. I'm lucky. Very, very lucky.

Wintery naked trees stood to attention in the still air, streetlights shone a welcoming shade of yellow, and when she passed a couple walking hand in hand along the footpath, they were smiling, their love for one another visible for all the world to see.

She pulled into the motel she and Lucy had stayed in only two weeks earlier, checked in, and sent Michael a text.

I'm here.

Fabulous. I've booked Anna's again for us. Pick you up in an hour?'

Sounds great. Room five. See you then.

On the dot of six-thirty, Michael's sleek silver BMW cruised into the motel car park and nosed into the visitor's bay.

As he approached her open door, Helen's beaming smile widened. For a few seconds they stood face to face, then he folded her in his arms and kissed her—gently at first, their lips barely touching, feeling each other's warmth. Then he leaned in, and she stepped back, closing the door behind him, cocooning him against her. They kissed again, this time firmly, passionately, until eventually she broke away, her eyes meeting his. 'Dinner first?'

He chuckled. 'I suppose so.'

She picked up her bag, tucked her hand into his, and they walked out into the night air, their warm breath creating frosty clouds in front of them.

THE FOLLOWING MORNING, still processing the information Michael had shared the previous night about his ex-wife's medical negligence claim, Helen got out of her car slowly. She was surprised at herself —and a little elated that she wasn't the only one to have suffered a challenging time. Somehow, Michael's story had made him more normal—less perfect—and weirdly, she liked that. She wasn't perfect. No one was. But knowing that Michael had also made mistakes strengthened her feelings for him.

She clicked the locking button and stowed her car key in her bag then paused mid-step as she stared at the crowd on the front veranda of the cottage—her cottage and her veranda.

'Welcome to your new house,' they chorused.

Tim and Heidi were there, Steve was standing behind Heidi's diminutive figure, and beside them, Lisa and Julian.

Michael's car drew up behind hers and he stepped out, a huge bunch of flowers in his hand. 'These are for you,' he said as he passed them to her and kissed her.

The others clapped and cheered as she took the bouquet and walked through the front gate. In the two weeks since she'd visited the house, the smell had lessened and the front lawn had sprouted hopeful new shoots of green.

'What are you all doing here?' She couldn't stop smiling. Having her family together and in front of what was now her own home was more than she could have wished for.

'We're waiting for the truck and will help you unpack,' Tim said.

'Julian and I've done a big grocery shop, so we won't go hungry,' Lisa added.

'I've got my swag too, Mum,' Steve said. 'Got permission to land the chopper on the farm next door, so if you need anything doing over the weekend, I'm at your disposal.'

Everyone laughed and Helen thought she might burst with happiness. She held up a set of keys tied together with a piece of red ribbon. 'Shall I go first?'

'Allow me,' Michael said, taking the key from her fingers and pushing it into the lock, turning it, then stepping back for her to enter before him as the door swung open. Once again, the fragrance of newly lacquered timber greeted them.

Helen breathed in the scent and closed her eyes. She was home.

EPILOGUE

ive months later

The last of the spring flowers had wilted and summer charged in with a vengeance. Although it was nowhere close to the heat experienced in a Central Queensland summer, Helen stood and wiped the perspiration from her forehead.

Flowers surrounded her, their budding heads gracefully nodding on the top of long stems, ripe for picking. The months had passed quickly as her days filled with working alongside her new friends, Lauren and Harley, a young, enthusiastic couple with a bourgeoning flower nursery. While she'd learned when and what to plant and how to care for flowers of all shapes and sizes, she'd taken home the knowledge and experimented—all while receiving a wage which, while not enough to live lavishly on, was quite adequate to get by without having to dip into the sale money she had left.

Once a week, she cut bunches of flowers, herbs, and vegetables from the beds Michael helped her build and took them to town to sell at the Saturday markets. The proceeds went straight into her travel account—and were already almost enough to pay for another visit to Scotland.

Michael was loving his new position in the hospital. He still worked odd and sometimes long hours, but they were so different from his life in the Sydney hospital that he barely noticed. He had purchased a comfortable town house walking distance to the main street, cafés, and Quart Pot Creek where he and Helen regularly walked Floss, Helen's new companion—a seven-year-old border collie whose elderly owner had passed away, leaving Floss homeless.

They had talked about moving in together but, with the flowers and vegetables consuming much of Helen's time and the need for Michael to be close to the hospital, they had agreed to share what time they could and spend days off together at Helen's cottage. Those days were extra special, and they'd often welcome Lisa and Julian to join them on a hike in the Girraween National Park. Or now that the warm weather had arrived and rain had filled the creek at the bottom of the garden, they would plunge in for a refreshing—and quick—swim in the chilly water.

With Lisa's move to the Beaudesert Veterinary Practice, she and Julian had bought a small house on the edge of town where Bobbie would lay blissfully sleeping while they worked. In the evenings, he ran alongside Lisa as she cycled the country roads and in the early mornings, he accompanied Julian on a half hour jog.

Steve, too, had surprised Helen with more visits than usual—possibly something to do with the neighbouring farmer's daughter, who had returned home after a decade of overseas career commitments. They'd allowed him to park his helicopter on the flat paddock behind the woolshed in exchange for regular aerial views of their farm—and had seemingly welcomed him into their family.

Tim and Heidi were expecting their first child, and although they had said they had no intention of marrying, the pretty diamond ring on her finger during their latest visit hadn't gone unnoticed by Helen.

With the foliage packed into boxes and buckets of water, Helen lay them on the shelving she and Michael had built for the job in readiness for the following day's market. Then she trudged up the steps into the cosy country kitchen.

She pressed the buttons on the new coffee machine —a gift from Michael, waiting for the steamy liquid to fill her mug. Then she frothed the milk and added it before sitting down and reading the invitation again. It was accompanied with a delightful letter from Ingrid.

Dear Helen and Michael,

It is so good to hear your news via Lucy and know you're both happy in your new lives. Callum and I are looking forward to seeing you all for our wedding—apologies for it being in winter but if nothing else, it's such a quiet time of year we'll have no trouble finding days and evenings to spend together. And, of course, you might have a chance to experience your first white winter.

We've organised accommodation for you all so you won't have to worry about fighting the tourist queue for a comfy bed—not that it would be a problem in early March!

Can't wait to see you all—and meanwhile, you and Michael better brush up on your dancing. THERE WILL BE A CEILIDH!

Love and best wishes,

Ingrid and Callum

Helen smiled at it. Another trip to the Isle of Skye and a wonderful chance to be together with friends and family.

Only this time it would be even better than before.

There would be no injuries—she would make sure of that—and ... she would be with the man she loved.

Elation lifted her once again as her thoughts swung to Michael. Who could have guessed a year earlier, how much her life would change?

She had no regrets—only lessons learned, often

the hard way. But at least she'd learned them and now she'd been offered a second chance—with Michael.

Life is good—and it will get better. Of that, she was certain.

ALSO BY HEATHER REYBURN

Tullagulla Series

The Cedar Tree

The English Oak

The Pepperina Grove

A Tullagulla Christmas

Fantail Ridge Series

Peninsula Promises

The Lupin Fields

The Scent of Promise

Featherwood Falls Series

A Stranger in Featherwood Falls

Secrets in Featherwood Falls

Sparks Fly in Featherwood Falls

Clouds over Featherwood Falls

Coming Home to Featherwood Falls

A Festive Featherwood Falls

Outback Skye

Letters in Blue

Dust on the Heather

AFTERWORD

If you enjoyed this book, I would love you to leave a review on your preferred site. Reviews encourage authors to continue writing and also help other readers to find my books.

Thank you for reading "Dust on the Heather".

ACKNOWLEDGMENTS

Huge thanks go to my friends and family for the support, love and honest feedback you share. I couldn't do it without you—you keep me grounded and your love lifts me when I need it most.

Thank you to my wonderful writing group—Susan, Phillipa and Michelle. Your friendship, guidance and constant encouragement are more valuable than you could know.

To my other author friends, thank you for your generosity. You are such wonderful people and I'm proud to share my love of writing with you. Thank you especially to George Reynolds, author of "Walking with Wade" for sharing his beautiful book and vast knowledge of hiking in Scotland with me.

Thanks to my wonderful editors, Anna Bishop and Lauren Clarke (CreatingINK) and to my proof readers, Dianne, Jennifer and Julia.

And last but by no means least, thank you for reading my work, writing reviews and recommending my stories to others. Without you, there would be no books.

References: Walking with Wade by George Reynolds

LETTERS IN BLUE

From the sunburnt plains of Outback Australia to the misty shores of the Isle of Skye, two women's fates are intertwined by heartbreak, mystery, and the relentless pull of destiny.

2024: Ingrid Sloane is burnt-out. When the opportunity for a break from her nursing career in Australia finally arrives, she is drawn to visit the Isle of Skye, her grandmother's birthplace. But a chance meeting with Fergus, a local Scot, and his nephew, Callum, leads to an unexpected discovery—a bundle of pale blue aerogrammes. The suggestion of a long-lost love touches Ingrid, and with Callum's help, she embarks on a quest to reunite the authors of the intriguing letters.

1990: Lucy Pellegreen found the perfect life on the

Isle of Skye—a man she adored and a future brimming with possibilities. But when a family emergency sends her home to the Australian Outback, the precious letters from Scotland become the only reminder of the love waiting there. Before she can return, one tragic twist changes everything, leaving her lost to the past in more ways than one.

Will Ingrid's search for answers lead to her own happiness? Or is history doomed to repeat itself?